餐飲英語
異國美食情緣
1◯◯% romantic, absolutely delicious

帶著情感品嚐美食，即是 **「人間美味」**
用英語表達富情感意涵的美食，才算得上是 **「食尚」**

美食情緣 由美食情緣英語故事**強化大腦記憶連結**，再搭配美食重點介紹，
進一步擴充自己的**美食語彙庫**，成為**犀利餐飲高手**。

美食口說 規劃 **「一問三答」** 單元，面對相同的問題卻能有**三種不同思路**的回答，在**口試**、
口譯、工作和**旅遊**時，能以英語表達出獨特、個人化看法。

3個 **Must** (必看、必會、必讀)

美食家、外語
美食主持人必會

餐飲科系和自
助旅行者必讀

導遊、領隊和
口譯人員必看

MP3

Preface 作者序

　　還記得到俄羅斯旅遊回國後，姊姊看了我拍的相片，說了句：「妳根本是用味蕾記憶旅行嘛！」從前只覺得這句話充滿貶意，但漸漸的，我不得不承認此話不假。在菸味無所不在的俄羅斯街道上，享受著那一片油膩卻獨特的油炸包；在開往瑞典的渡輪上，因為口袋不深，只能邊望著豐盛的自助餐，邊啃著冷冰冰的芬蘭米派；在印度擁擠又喧囂的街上，炸脆餅小點的攤子讓我又好奇又害怕…。這種種的味蕾記憶，總讓我在回想起食物的味道和香氣時，在霎那間帶我回到旅程的途中。這次多虧倍斯特出版社賞識，能讓我以美食英語的形式，與各位讀者分享我的美食記憶。期盼各位在閱讀時，能獲得一些學英文的樂趣，並燃起品嘗美食的渴望，這樣，就不枉本書的誕生了。

怡歆

Editor's 編者序

　　飲食與生活息息相關，而品嚐美食更是人生一大樂事。同樣的食物在不同文化影響與時間進展下演變出別具特色的美食，甚至在旅行時讓人感到別具異國風味。

　　在國外，富含異國風情的美食跟地域特色，帶給遊客、留學生們更多新鮮感跟刺激，有時候也成了愛情的催化劑，發展成一段美食良緣。書籍中第一部分先以浪漫的美食情緣故事引入主題，讓讀者用輕鬆的方式學習美食語彙，並由美食特色介紹進一步了解美食特點。第二部分則規劃了『一問三答』單元，在應答上提供三種不同思路：❶愛玩咖 Michelle：無厘頭、妙語連珠、犀利、又帶點詼諧。❷冒險王 Matt：中肯、實際、魅力十足的背包客。❸小資女 Becca：富創意、趣味性十足、具個人特色。讀者能由這些思路強化自己的英語表達能力，更具體表達出自己品嚐美食後的感受，並根據自己的口感、喜好等等調整成適合自己的答案，讓不管是面試官或外籍友人都對您更另眼相看，像是哇！*full of personality*（充滿個性），*a little bit charm*（有些許魅力），*not memorization*（不是背誦），*dull*（沉悶的）等等的。所以還等什麼呢?趕快感受一下美食威力，體驗全新的餐飲英語學習，Let's Go!!!

編輯部敬上

目次
CONTENTS

part 1 美食異國情緣篇

美洲

1. Clam Chowder 蛤蠣巧達湯（美國）*012*

2. Muffin 馬芬蛋糕（美國）*016*

3. Cranberry Bread 蔓越莓麵包（美國）*020*

4. Mashed Potato 馬鈴薯泥（美國）*024*

5. Boston Lobster 波士頓龍蝦（美國）*028*

6. Mac'n Cheese 奶醬通心粉（美國）*032*

7. Tuna Melt Sandwich 熱烤鮪魚起司三明治（美國）*036*

8. Apple Pie 蘋果派（美國）*040*

9. Cornbread 玉米麵包（墨西哥、美國）*044*

10. Nachos 焗烤玉米片（墨西哥、美國）*048*

11. Chili 辣豆燉肉（墨西哥）*052*

12. Tortilla Chips 墨西哥玉米片（墨西哥）*056*

亞洲

13. Falafel 中東蔬菜球（土耳其及中東）*060*

14. Pani Puri 炸脆餅小點（印度）*064*

15. Biriyani 香料炒飯（印度）068

16. Green Papaya Salad 青木瓜沙拉（泰國）072

17. Pineapple Bun with Butter 冰火菠蘿油（香港）076

18. Oden 關東煮（日本）080

19. Tamagoyaki 玉子燒（日本）084

20. Rice Cake 年糕（台灣）088

21. Satay 沙嗲串燒（印尼）092

22. Century Egg and Tofu 皮蛋豆腐（台灣）096

23. Daikon Cake 蘿蔔糕（台灣、香港）100

歐洲

24. Beef Tartare 韃靼牛肉（法國）104

25. Hot chocolate 熱巧克力（法國）108

26. Duck à l'orange 柳橙鴨（法國）112

27. Croque Madame 焗烤火腿乳酪吐司（法國）116

28. Fish and Chips 炸魚薯條（英國）120

29. Cottage Pie 農舍派（愛爾蘭、英國）124

30. Karelian pasty 米派（芬蘭）128

31. Salmon Chowder with Dill 鮭魚蒔蘿濃湯（瑞典）132

32. Waffle 格子鬆餅（比利時）*136*

33. Stroopwafel 焦糖煎餅（荷蘭）*140*

34. Borscht 羅宋湯（俄國）*144*

35. Danish Pastry 丹麥麵包（奧地利）*148*

36. Frankfurter Sausage 法蘭克福香腸（德國）*152*

37. Flaki 牛肚湯（波蘭）*156*

38. Churro 吉拿棒（西班牙）*160*

39. Tomato Garlic Bread 番茄大蒜麵包（西班牙）*164*

40. Sachertorte 薩赫蛋糕（奧地利）*168*

41. Pirozhki 油炸包（俄國）*172*

42. Cinnamon Roll 肉桂捲（芬蘭）*176*

43. Semifreddo 冰淇淋凍糕（義大利）*180*

44. Herring Sandwich 鯡魚三明治（荷蘭）*184*

45. Croquette 可樂餅（義大利）*188*

澳洲

46. Flat White 牛奶濃縮咖啡（澳洲）*192*

47. Vegemite 維吉麥抹醬（澳洲）*196*

48. Pavlova 帕洛瓦蛋糕（紐西蘭）*200*

part2 美食口語強化篇 💬

美洲

1. Steak in Blue Cheese Sauce 藍紋起司醬牛排（美國）*206*

2. Barbecue Pork Ribs 炭烤肋排（美國）*208*

3. Fish Sticks 炸魚條（美國）*210*

4. California Roll 加州捲（美國）*212*

5. Chicken Pot Pie 雞肉深鍋派（美國）*214*

6. Cronut 可拿滋（美國）*216*

7. Cupcake 杯子蛋糕（美國）*218*

歐洲

8. Frog Legs 蛙腿（法國）*220*

9. Escargot 烤蝸牛（法國）*222*

10. Roulade de Volaille 雞肉捲（法國）*224*

11. Jellied Eel 鰻魚凍（英國）*226*

12. Corned Beef 鹽醃牛肉（愛爾蘭）*228*

13. Polenta 玉米粥（義大利）*230*

14. Eggplant Parmesan 焗烤千層茄（義大利）*232*

15. Ravioli 義大利餃（義大利）*234*

16. Schweinshaxe 德國豬腳（德國）*236*

17. Pierogi 波蘭餃（波蘭）*238*

18. Cheese Fondue 起士鍋（瑞士）*240*

19. Yorkshire pudding 約克夏布丁（英國）*242*

20. Kebab 串烤（中東）*244*

21. Baklava 果仁蜜餅（希臘、土耳其）*246*

22. French Toast 法式吐司（法國、德國等）*248*

23. Salmiakki 甘草糖（北歐）*250*

24. Pastel de Nata 葡式蛋塔（葡萄牙）*252*

25. Nougat 牛軋糖（西班牙）*254*

26. Crêpe 可麗餅（法國）*256*

27. Crème Brûlée 烤布蕾（法國）*258*

28. Macaron 馬卡龍（法國）*260*

美洲

29. Naan 南餅（印度）*262*

30. Sashimi 生魚片（日本）*264*

31. Nattō 納豆（日本）*266*

32. Minced Pork Rice 滷肉飯（台灣）268

33. Bak kut the 肉骨茶（馬來西亞）270

34. Samgyetang 人參雞湯（韓國）272

35. General Tso's Chicken 左宗棠雞（中國）274

36. Xiaolongbao 小籠包（中國）276

37. Pad Thai 泰式炒河粉（泰國）278

38. Dango 糰子（日本）280

39. Tanghulu 糖葫蘆（中國）282

澳洲 --

40. Meat Pie 肉派（澳洲）284

美食達人得分表

♡12~14 美食新手　　♡24~36 小小美食家　　♡48 頂級美食達人

美洲 ---

♡ 1. 蛤蠣巧達湯（美國）

♡ 2. 馬芬蛋糕（美國）

♡ 3. 蔓越莓麵包（美國）

♡ 4. 馬鈴薯泥（美國）

♡ 5. 波士頓龍蝦（美國）

♡ 6. 奶醬通心粉（美國）

♡ 7. 熱烤鮪魚起司三明治（美國）

♡ 8. 蘋果派（美國）

♡ 9. 玉米麵包（墨西哥、美國）

♡ 10. 焗烤玉米片（墨西哥、美國）

♡ 11. 辣豆燉肉（墨西哥）

♡ 12. 墨西哥玉米片（墨西哥）

亞洲 ---

♡ 13. 中東蔬菜球（土耳其及中東）

♡ 14. 炸脆餅小點（印度）

♡ 15. 香料炒飯（印度）

♡ 16. 青木瓜沙拉（泰國）

♡ 17. 冰火菠蘿油（香港）

♡ 18. 關東煮（日本）

♡ 19. 玉子燒（日本）

♡ 20. 年糕（台灣）

♡ 21. 沙嗲串燒（印尼）

♡ 22. 皮蛋豆腐（台灣）

♡ 23. 蘿蔔糕（台灣、香港）

歐洲 ---

♡ 24. 韃靼牛肉（法國）

♡ 25. 熱巧克力（法國）

♡ 26. 柳橙鴨（法國）

♡ 27. 焗烤火腿乳酪吐司（法國）

♡ 28. 炸魚薯條（英國）

♡ 29. 農舍派（愛爾蘭、英國）

♡ 30. 米派（芬蘭）

♡ 31. 鮭魚蒔蘿濃湯（瑞典）

♡ 32. 格子鬆餅（比利時）

♡ 33. 焦糖煎餅（荷蘭）

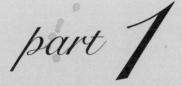

part 1

美食異國情緣篇

♡ 34. 羅宋湯（俄國）

♡ 35. 丹麥麵包（奧地利）

♡ 36. 法蘭克福香腸（德國）

♡ 37. 牛肚湯（波蘭）

♡ 38.吉拿棒（西班牙）

♡ 39.番茄大蒜麵包（西班牙）

♡ 40.薩赫蛋糕（奧地利）

♡ 41.油炸包（俄國）

♡ 42.肉桂捲（芬蘭）

♡ 43.冰淇淋凍糕（義大利）

♡ 44.鯡魚三明治（荷蘭）

♡ 45.可樂餅（義大利）

澳洲 -----------------------------------

♡ 46.牛奶濃縮咖啡（澳洲）

♡ 47.維吉麥抹醬（澳洲）

♡ 48.帕洛瓦蛋糕（紐西蘭）

看完了也別忘了……塗鴉愛心符號喔！

unit 1

Clam Chowder
蛤蠣巧達湯

 情緣園地 MP3 *01*

Finally, I'm here – the **historical** city of **the States**, Boston. It **depressed** me to **travel** alone **for business** in this beautiful city at first. However, after I arrived, the fresh air and **delightful breeze** welcomed me just like my **beloved** baby girl. Now I'm sitting here **sipping on** my creamy clam chowder, feeling the sunshine and the smell of sea water.

My baby girl loves sea food. I remember our first date in a seafood restaurant. She was **impressed** by the way I opened up a lobster. How wonderful would it be if she could be here with me? The chowder is full of flavor; I can almost taste the ocean down there in my bowl. The cream is like an **embrace** to my body. It is thick and warm, so hearty and so comforting.

　　我總算到這兒來了，美國歷史悠久的都市──波士頓。本來要自己來這個美麗的城市出差還挺讓我沮喪的，不過，抵達之後的清新空氣和令人愉快的微風讓我覺得賓至如歸，就像我心愛的女孩在這兒歡迎我似的。現在，我邊坐在這兒品嘗蛤蠣巧達湯，邊享受陽光和海洋的氣息。

　　我的女孩最喜歡海鮮，還記得第一次約會我們在一家海鮮餐館，她對我獨到的開龍蝦方式大感驚奇。如果她能跟我一起來這兒該有多好呢？這道湯滋味馥郁，我甚至覺得在碗裡品嘗了整個海洋。奶油像擁抱般包裹我，既濃稠又溫暖，十足暖心且令人放鬆。

◉ Clam chowder

A very creamy soup made of clams, onions, milk and cream. It is usually served in a bread bowl, which is a rounded **crusty** bread emptied inside. The soup will be poured in and served in the bread, topped with **crackers** to give it more texture. Many will only drink the soup and leave the bread, since it is usually considered a container. But the bread is also **edible** and it's good after it **absorbs** all the **goodness** in the soup. One can taste the saltiness of the clam and the sweetness of the cream **altogether** in the **moist** and **fluffy** bread.

◉ 蛤蠣巧達湯

這是一道由蛤蠣、洋蔥、鮮奶和奶油為主組成的濃郁湯品，通常是由外皮脆硬、裡面挖空的麵包碗裡盛著湯的方式呈現。濃湯會裝在麵包碗裡，並灑上餅乾增添口感。很多人只喝湯而不吃外面的麵包，因為麵包看起來就只是個容器罷了。其實麵包也可以食用，而且在吸收了湯汁之後非常美味；在濕潤且蓬鬆的麵包體裡嘗得到蛤蠣的鹹和奶油的甜。

字彙補充包

historical **adj** 歷史悠久的	the States　美國的別稱
depress **v** 使沮喪	travl for business　出差
delightful **adj** 令人愉快的	breeze **n** 微風
sip on　啜飲	impressed **adj** 印象深刻的
embrace **v** 擁抱	hearty **adj** 暖心的
comforting **adj** 撫慰人的	crusty **adj** 硬皮的
cracker **n** 脆餅	edible **adj** 可食用的
absorb **v** 吸收	goodness **n** 精華
altogether **adv** 一同	moist **adj** 濕潤的
fluffy **adj** 蓬鬆的	belovd **adj** 深愛的

Muffin
馬芬蛋糕

 情緣園地 MP3 ▸ 02

To truly enjoy a cup of **drip** black coffee, you must have someone to **accompany** you. There were mornings when I spent time in a local coffee shop – it was hard to get my husband up early so it was usually just me – to have a cup of drip black coffee and a chocolate chip muffin.

I'm **no big fan** of chocolate, but my husband definitely has a **sweet tooth**. He loves chocolate, especially a moist, **melt-in-the-mouth** chocolate chip muffin. I used to **tease** him for being such a sugar **maniac**, but to be honest, I have to admit that a nice sweet chocolate chip muffin goes well with drip black coffee. For some reason, they just **click** perfectly, and so do we.

要真正享受一杯濾泡式黑咖啡，我必須有伴。有些早晨我會在當地的咖啡廳消磨時間——要外子早起很難，所以常常是我獨自前往——享受一杯濾泡式黑咖啡，還有一個巧克力碎片瑪芬。

我不是很喜歡巧克力，但外子頗嗜甜食。他愛死了巧克力，尤其是濕潤、入口即化的巧克力碎片瑪芬。我以前曾笑他是吃糖的螞蟻，但坦白說，我必須承認一個甜美的巧克力碎片瑪芬跟濾泡式黑咖啡真的很搭。毫無緣由的，它們就是合拍，就跟我倆一樣。

 **美食重點介紹**

Muffin

Unlike cupcakes, these breakfast treats don't look fancy. Nevertheless, they are morning essentials for many. In coffee shops especially, they pretty much play a leading role. Although they look simple and rustic, muffins are super moist inside. The flavors of muffins are huge: from lemon poppy seed, apple cinnamon, to blueberry, or the classical chocolate chip: the variation goes on and on. It is a convenient food as well, since one can just grab it and rush to work, without worrying about the icing ruining one's office suit. Just like how simple they look, muffins are easy to make too!

◉ 瑪芬蛋糕

不若杯子蛋糕花俏奪目，瑪芬蛋糕看起來十分樸實。雖說如此，瑪芬對許多人來說卻是早晨必需品。特別在咖啡館，瑪芬可說是獨領風騷。儘管外觀簡樸又單純，卻有濕潤無比的內在。瑪芬口味眾多，從檸檬罌粟籽、蘋果肉桂、到藍莓或經典巧克力碎片，變化可以無限延伸。瑪芬同時也是十分方便的食物，趕著上班時，你可以抓了就走，不必擔心蛋糕糖霜弄髒襯衫。就如其簡樸的外觀，瑪芬的作法也是簡單到家。

 字彙補充包

accompany **v** 陪伴		no big fan 不喜歡…	
sweet tooth 甜食愛好者		melt-in-the-mouth 入口即化的	
tease **v** 嘲弄		maniac **n** 狂熱者	
they click（兩個人）一拍即合		brewer **n** 咖啡館	
nevertheless **adv** 然而		essential **adj** 必須的	
leading role **n** 主角		rustic **adj** 農村的	
classical **adj** 經典的		variation **n** 多樣性	
grab **v** 抓住		icing **n** 糖霜	
ruin **v** 損壞		unlike 不像…	
drip **v** 滴漏			

Part **1** 美食異國情緣篇

Part **2** 美食口語強化篇

Cranberry Bread
蔓越莓麵包

unit 3

Have you ever tasted cranberries? They are **tangy** and a little bit sweet. It's like life, sometimes sweet but usually **sour**. Some people add a lot of sugar and make it into **preserves**. I don't. I like to taste the **original** flavor, knowing that the reality is **harsh**. However, cranberry bread is a good way to eat cranberries. The bread itself is **firm** to touch, not too sweet but filling. Very **down to earth**, I would say. Hank is not a fan of cranberry. Not at all. When he sees me eating it, he never wants a slice.

Today we have lunch break together, but I somewhat feel that he is not **at ease**. **As usual**, I pull out my loaf of **homemade** cranberry bread and start slicing it. Oh boy this looks great. Hmm, yummy... Is that Hank talking to me? Ouh, the tanginess, yes. He is saying something about me being beautiful **and stuff**, is he serious? This thing is so good, I can't stop eating it. Is he talking about getting married now? **No kidding**.

　　曾吃過蔓越莓麵包嗎？蔓越莓嘗起來酸澀微甜，好像人生一般，常時苦澀，有時甜美。有人會加糖將蔓越莓作成果醬，我卻不好此道；我喜歡品嘗蔓越莓的原味，這讓我知道現實是嚴峻的。不過呢，蔓越莓麵包倒是不錯的選擇。麵包體本身十分紮實，嘗來不過甜，且十分有飽足感，有一種踏實的感覺。漢克不喜歡蔓越莓，徹底的不喜歡。當他看到我在吃蔓越莓麵包時，他從來未曾開口要一片共享。

　　今天我們一起吃午餐，不知怎地，我感到他似乎有些不自在。我一如往常地拿出自製蔓越莓麵包，並開始切片。哇賽，這看起來真好吃。嗯～美味。漢克是在跟我講話嗎？噢，就是這股酸勁兒，太棒了。他在說什麼我真是有女人味又有魅力之類的，真的假的啊？這真美味，停不下來呢。他現在是在跟我求婚嗎？

● Cranberry bread

Despite its name "bread", cranberry bread is not made of bread flour. **Rather**, it's more like a firm cake. In the United States, this kind of "cake" is called quick bread, which means a **dough** with no yeast. Banana bread, carrot bread and zucchini bread are also **of this kind**. In general, cranberry bread is less sweet and more **solid** than the other ones. Berries are usually picked during summer time and **stored** for winter. They can be frozen, **canned**, or made into dry goods for longer preservation. Tasting the berries in **pastries** is actually the experience of biting into the riches of the season.

● 蔓越莓麵包

雖其名為「麵包」，但實際上蔓越莓麵包並非使用高筋麵粉製成。相反的，其感覺較接近蛋糕。在美國，這種「蛋糕」被稱為快速麵包，意思是無添加酵母的麵包。香蕉麵包、胡蘿蔔麵包和櫛瓜麵包皆屬此類。一般來說，蔓越莓麵包比起上述其他而言味道較不甜，且結構更紮實。莓果類常是於夏季。採收並存放至冬季，儲存方式有冷凍、醃漬、或做成乾料好存放得更久。品嘗糕點中的莓果是一種大口咬下當季鮮美的體驗。

字彙補充包

tangy	adj 酸澀的	sour	adj 酸的、n 酸味
preserve	n 果醬、醃漬品	original	adj 起初、原初的
firm	adj 紮實的	down to earth	腳踏實地的
homemade	adj 自製的	at ease	感覺自在
as usual	如往常一般	and stuff	…之類的
no kidding	不會吧；怎麼可能	despite	儘管
Rather	而是…	of this kind	像這類的
solid	adj 硬、實在的	store	v 保存
can	v 裝罐、醃漬	pastry	n 糕點
harsh	adj 嚴峻的	dough	n （麵包的）麵團

23

unit 4

Mashed Potato
馬鈴薯泥

 情緣園地 MP3 04

The first time I tasted his perfectly mashed potatoes was on a normal day. I accidently stepped in a **diner** that I didn't plan to go to. What happened was **a row of coincidences**: the chicken salad that I wanted was **sold out**, so I had a steak instead. And there it was – the little scoop of mashed potato sitting beside the steak, so clean and **elegant**.

It was like the **fireworks** of the **fourth of July** in my head. It just **exploded** when I took it in my mouth. Then I totally **ignored** the steak and just **stared** at that mashed potato. It was hard to find out who made this, I said to myself, and I told the waiter to call the cook. There he was, Joana. It was a dream come true. The smooth mashed potato was like a **slide** that took me to simple happiness.

　　我與完美的馬鈴薯泥相遇在一個普通的日子，那天我意外的踏入一間我沒想過要去的餐館用餐，接著發生的事是一連串的巧合：我想點的雞肉沙拉賣完了，所以我改點牛排。就是那客牛排——旁邊有一勺馬鈴薯泥，白淨又優雅的放在那兒。

　　當我吃下一口馬鈴薯泥，它就像國慶煙火般在我腦海中綻放。接著牛排便被我完全無視，我只能緊盯著那團馬鈴薯泥。很難察覺出這是誰做的，我心想，然後我請服務生叫廚師來。接著，約拿出現了。這真是夢想成真。綿密軟糯的馬鈴薯泥是一道滑梯，帶我滑入純粹的幸福。

美食重點介紹

● Mashed Potato

The **ultimate** comfort food of many, mashed potato plays an **indispensable supporting role** in many main dishes, especially those with **gravy**. The key to perfect mashed potato is the fat – melted butter and light cream will do a good job adding **smoothness** to it and balancing the flavor at the same time. Potatoes need to be **thoroughly** cooked, drained and seasoned properly. Neither the saltiness nor the sweetness should **triumph** one another. Sometimes, if mashed potato is served alone, herbs like thyme, basil or oregano may be applied for a different taste.

● 馬鈴薯泥

對很多人來說，馬鈴薯泥是終極的心靈撫慰食物，是很多主菜不可或缺的邊菜，特別是那些有肉汁的主食。製作完美馬鈴薯泥的訣竅是油脂：融化奶油和鮮奶油非常適合，它們會在帶來柔順口感的同時平衡整體的滋味。馬鈴薯必須被煮透、徹底瀝乾並適度調味，鹹味和甜味應彼此平衡，而非有其中一個特別突出。若馬鈴薯泥單獨做一道菜，有時候也加入像百里香、羅勒或奧勒岡等香草，用以產生不同的味道。

字彙補充包

foamy **adj** 綿密的	ideal **adj** 理想中的
diner **n** 小餐館	a row of 一連串的
coincidence **n** 巧合	sell out 售罄、賣光
elegant **adj** 優雅的	firework **n** 煙火
fourth of July 美國國慶日	explode **v** 爆炸
ignore **v** 忽略	stare **v** 盯著
slide **n** 溜滑梯	ultimate **adj** 終極的、最終的
indispensable **adj** 不可或缺的	supporting role **n** 配角
gravy **n** 肉汁	smoothness **n** 滑順
thoroughly **adv** 透徹地	triumph **v** 勝出

Boston Lobster
波士頓龍蝦

情緣園地 MP3 05

After Laura recommends me to give it a try, I'm dying to know how a bland carcass in a shell can be so famous. It's actually an experience of luxurious delicate taste of meat, something a meat-and-potato Texan knows absolutely nothing about.

So there it is, a whole boiled lobster in its shell on the dining table. Laura carefully shows me how to open the shells with the scissors and **pliers**. It requires patience and prudence to eat this meal, and as I **gaze at** every single **movement** Laura makes, I realize that it's not just about the **appearance**. Every effort one pays to **accomplish** a mission will make the fruit tastier, and so shall it be our relationship. As for the lobster itself? I'd say it **lives up to its fame**.

　　蘿拉推薦我嘗嘗後，我也很想知道一個平淡無味的甲殼類到底是為什麼能這麼有名。這是奢華細緻的肉品體驗，一個對德州佬全然陌生的東西。

　　上菜了，一隻完整的水煮龍蝦被端上桌了。蘿拉小心翼翼的示範如何用剪刀和鉗子開龍蝦殼，吃這道菜還真需要耐心和細心哩。當我注視著蘿拉的每個小動作時，我才發現外表不是決定一切的因素──為完成一件事所付出的努力才能使果實更加甜美，而我們的關係也應該如此。至於龍蝦滋味如何？我倒是必須說不辱其名呢。

● Boston lobster

Thanks to its **geographic vantage**, Boston is **gifted with** the fruits of sea. It is **no surprise** that lobster has become one of the most famous dishes in the New England area. The most common ways lobsters are prepared are boiled, steamed or stuffed. Boiled lobster is usually dipped into melted butter, and **accompanied with** coleslaw and fries. Stuffed lobster is fried, chopped and **refilled** into its shell. Also, lobsters are shredded and mixed with mayonnaise, which is known as lobster salad. Lobsters, prepared any way, are a proud tradition for many New Englanders.

● 波士頓龍蝦

多虧了地域優勢，波士頓有相當多的海產。因此，龍蝦成為新英格蘭地區最有名的菜色之一，也不令人意外了。龍蝦最常見的料理方式為：水煮、蒸煮或填餡。水煮的龍蝦要沾融化的奶油，並搭配捲心菜沙拉和薯條。填餡龍蝦則是先炒過，將肉切好後再填回龍蝦殼中。當然，龍蝦肉也會被撕碎並與美乃滋混合，這就是著名的龍蝦沙拉。不管哪種料理方式，龍蝦都是新英格蘭地區居民引以為傲的傳統菜。

字彙補充包

Texan **n** 德州人	luxurious **adj** 奢華的
be dying to know 非常想知道…	carcass **n** 屍骸
plier **n** 鉗子	gaze at 定睛注視…
movement **n** 動作	appearance **n** 外表、外貌
accomplish **v** 達成、完成	live up to its fame 不辱其名、名實相符
geographic **adj** 地理上的	vantage **n** 優勢、優點
be gifted with 有…的恩賜／天分	no surprise 不意外地
be accompanied with 由…陪伴著	refill **v** 再裝入、填入

unit 6

Mac 'n Cheese
奶醬通心粉

Inviting Jason to my place made me nervous. So I still have two hours before dinner and I have macaroni and cheddar cheese here...what else do I need? Greens. Yes. We need to **go healthy**. There is some frozen broccoli in the freezer. Perfect.

What should I do with them though? Oh, I should **thaw** them in the microwave... okay. So I'm gonna cook this macaroni and mix it with cheese sauce... right, that looks good. To the oven. Now, the broccoli is done too, it is hot and **steaming**. Looking good. I've got some good **silverware** here. I hope it's not **over the top** for this **occasion**. Anyway. The mac 'n cheese is done, what a smell! Hmm... wait, I only got fifteen minutes left? No way! I haven't gotten dressed! Is that the doorbell ringing? Oh, come on! You can't be serious!

　　邀請傑森到我家裡來讓我很緊張。距離晚餐還有兩小時，通心粉和切達起司也準備好了。我還需要什麼？綠色蔬菜，對了，我們走健康路線。冷凍庫裡有花椰菜，完美。

　　我該拿它們怎麼辦？喔，我要拿到微波爐去解凍…好。現在我要煮通心粉，然後把它跟起司醬混合在一塊…好，看起來很棒，現在進烤箱。花椰菜也準備好了，還冒著熱煙呢。我有些銀製餐具，希望看起來不會太假掰。隨便啦。奶醬通心粉做好了，聞起來真香！嗯…等等，我只剩十五分鐘？不可能！我還沒換衣服耶！那是電鈴在響嗎？吼！怎麼會這樣啦！

美食重點介紹

● Mac 'n cheese

Short for "macaroni and cheese", mac 'n cheese is a household dish for every American family. As simple as it sounds, all one has to do is to cook the macaroni, make the creamy and cheesy sauce, top it with bread crumbs and bake it. Before you know it, the dish is done! And everyone loves it. It is almost magical. Mac 'n cheese is considered a comfort food for many Americans, as well as an old-fashioned American classic. The creamy sauce may be a little bit too rich for some, so to give it a twist, some paprika or chili powder may do the job.

● 奶醬通心粉

Mac 'n cheese 是通心粉 macaroni 和起司 cheese 的縮寫，這是一道美國家喻戶曉的菜餚。誠如其名，料理這道菜只需煮好通心粉、製作起司醬，並撒上麵包粉烘烤就行了。幾分鐘後，料理完成了！而且人見人愛，簡直像施魔法一樣。奶醬通心粉被很多美國人認為是撫慰身心的料理，這也是一道老式經典美國菜。對有些人來說，起司醬可能太過濃郁，為使整道菜多點層次，可以加些匈牙利紅椒粉或辣椒粉。

字彙補充包

gosh　天哪	have a crush on　愛上某人
semester　n 學期	go healthy　走健康路線
thaw　v 解凍	steaming　adj 冒煙的
silverware　n 銀製餐具	over the top　太超過；浮誇
occasion　n 場合	you can't be serious 不可能；不會吧
household　adj 家喻戶曉的	top　v 把⋯放在上面
crumb　n 碎屑	before you know it 指很短的時間內
magical　adj 魔法般的	be considered + n 被認為是
comfort food　撫慰身心的食物	old-fashioned adj 老式；舊時代的
twist　v 扭轉	do the job　奏效

unit 7

Tuna Melt Sandwich
熱烤鮪魚起司三明治

 情緣園地 MP3 *07*

Peep. You've got one message. It's her, Esther. I know what she wants even without reading the **SMS**: a tuna melt sandwich. Esther is my neighbor, and we have known each other since we were in the **cradle**. Her parents are looking at me like we are already **an item**, and so are mine. As a **full-grown** man in his 20s, I gotta say I want her so bad. However, since her **attitude** is an always changing **mirage**, I figured that it's better to just **lay low** and wait.

Esther enjoys the hot melting cheese on tuna so much, that just watching her eating gives me **pleasure**. I've tried to **talk her into** a steak or a meatball sandwich, but she always says "the old way is the best way". Today I'm giving her some **extra** tuna, hoping that inside of the simple goodness she can taste a hint of my affection. There she comes, grinning from ear to ear. "You are the old one and the best one." She says. As I hand over the sandwich to her, I feel myself handing over a part of my heart to her too.

嗶。您有一則新訊息，是伊斯特。我不用看就知道她要什麼：一個熱烤鮪魚起司三明治。伊斯特是我的鄰居，我們從還在搖籃裡的時候就認識彼此了。她的父母早把我跟她看做一對，我的父母也一樣。對我這個成熟的二十幾歲男人來説，我很想跟她在一起。但因著她的態度仍舊曖昧不明，我覺得還是低調等待比較聰明。

伊斯特很喜歡熱烤鮪魚起司三明治，光看她吃就覺得幸福。我曾想説服她嘗試牛排三明治或肉丸三明治，但她總是説「老派最棒了」。今天我在三明治裡加了多一點點的鮪魚，希望她在簡單的美味中嘗到我對她的心意。她帶著燦爛的笑容走過來了，「你是老朋友，也是最好的朋友。」她説。當我將三明治交給她時，我感到自己把一部份的心也交出去了。

Tuna melt sandwich

Tuna melt is one of the most typical American sandwiches. Based on tuna salad, it is constituted of layers of lettuce and cheese. The word "melt" comes from the way it is heated up: usually, the sandwich is grilled or pressed in a panini machine. As a result, the bread is pressed down, squeezing out the melted, almost fluid cheese, which makes it extremely appetizing. The same method can be applied to turkey, ham or other sliced deli meats. The turkey melt sandwich and the tuna melt sandwich are all-time favorites on the menus of many cafés and at Subway.

熱烤鮪魚三明治

鮪魚三明治可說是最典型的美式三明治之一。三明治以鮪魚沙拉為基礎，再加上一層層的萵苣起士。「熱烤」這詞源自加熱的方式；通常三明治會被放在燒烤架上或是帕尼尼機裡，當麵包體被擠壓時，融化起士流瀉而出，看起來極為誘人。鮪魚沙拉也可替換為火雞肉、火腿或其他熟食肉類的薄片。熱烤火雞肉三明治和熱烤鮪魚三明治是咖啡廳和 Subway 的固定菜單。

字彙補充包

SMS　n　手機簡訊

an item　一對；情侶

attitude　n 態度

lay low　低調；低姿態

talk sb. into sth.
說服某人做某事

a hint of　一絲；一點點

grin from ear to ear
形容笑容燦爛

based on　建立在…之上

layer　n 層

squeeze　v 擠、壓

cradle　n 搖籃

full-grown　adj 成熟的；長成的

mirage　n 幻象；海市蜃樓

pleasure　n 喜悅

extra　adj 額外的

affection　n 愛慕；情意

hand over　交出

be constituted of　由…構成

come from　以…為由來

fluid　adj 流動的

Part **1** 美食異國情緣篇

Part **2** 美食口語強化篇

Apple Pie
蘋果派

 情緣園地 MP3 08

I hate exams. **Finance** is absolutely **devastating**. After I stepped out of the classroom, I felt that I was gonna **collapse**. I remember Alex followed me out and **dragged** me by my arms. He said something about getting coffee, and curiously here I am, in his apartment. Alex is a cute guy, **not quite** my dream man, but not bad. I know he has been **hitting on** me for months, but... Anyway, the hot tea in my hand is fixing my exam anxiety, and that's nice.

I smell something very **fragrant**, is that cinnamon? Something buttery and surgery... There he is, Alex is **grinning** and holding a plate. What is that? It's an apple pie! I can't believe this, did he make it himself? Let me have a bite first... hmmm! That's yummy! Maybe he thinks that I am **easy to charm**, but I don't really care. If he can make this for me whenever I am down, deal.

　　我恨考試。財經真是讓我沮喪。走出教室的時候，我覺得我要崩潰了。艾力克斯好像跟著我出來，還抓著我的手臂說去喝杯咖啡什麼的，結果我現在竟然在他的公寓了。艾力克斯是很可愛沒錯，但不算我的夢中情人，就還不錯啦。我知道他幾個月前就迷上我了，但…不管啦，至少這杯熱茶安撫了我因考試而焦躁的心。

　　我好像聞到什麼很香的味道，是肉桂嗎？什麼東西充滿奶油和糖…噢，艾力克斯帶著微笑現身了，他拿著個盤子。那是什麼？是個蘋果派耶！該不會是他自己做的吧？我簡直不敢相信。先來吃吃看吧…哇！超好吃！他可能覺得我還滿好到手的，但沒差啦，我不在乎。如果每次我沮喪他都做蘋果派給我吃，OK 啊。

美食重點介紹

● Apple pie

There are all different kinds of apple pies all over the world, and the most famous one might be McDonald's deep fried apple pie. Unsurprisingly, apple pie turns out to be one of the most American things one can possibly think of. There was even a saying that during World War Two, an apple pie could instantly make an American soldier cry out of homesickness. In France, Normandy apple tart is another interpretation of apple pie with no upper crust. It is usually served with whipped cream or ice cream. In Poland, apple pie is made in three layers: lower crust, shredded apple and meringue.

● 蘋果派

世界各地有各式各樣不同的蘋果派，而其中最為人知的當屬麥當勞的油炸蘋果派。若說蘋果派是最美式的食物之一，也不令人意外。甚至曾有人說，第二次世界大戰時，一個蘋果派可以立刻讓美國大兵因想家而哭出來。在法國，無上蓋的諾曼地蘋果塔是蘋果派的另一種詮釋。打發鮮奶油或冰淇淋常拿來和蘋果派做搭配。在波蘭，蘋果派被做成三層：酥底、蘋果絲夾層和蛋白霜頂。

字彙補充包

finance **n** 財經	drag **v** 拖；拉
collapse **v** 崩潰；倒塌	hit on sb. 喜歡上某人
not quite 不算是…	fragrant **adj** 芬芳的
grin **v** 咧嘴笑	easy to charm 形容女孩容易追到手
down **adj** 心情沮喪的	deal **n** 成交
unsurprisingly **adv** 不令人意外地	turn out 結果是…
saying **n** 說法	soldier **n** 士兵
homesickness **n** 思鄉病	interpretation **n** 詮釋
upper **adj** 上層的	shredded **adj** 銼絲的
devastating **adj** 毀滅性的	

Cornbread
玉米麵包

9

 情緣園地 MP3 09

I met Paula in a **potluck** home party. She was nothing special: not **stunningly** beautiful, not **unexpectedly** smart or **humorous**. In a word: **ordinary**. I didn't notice her **for the better part of** the party, because, hm, normal guys **tend to** talk to attractive ladies, right? After I had a few conversations with some girls, I headed back to the dining room for some snacks. On the table, **aside from** canapés and cocktail shrimp, I **spotted** cornbread. I grabbed one and returned to the inner room.

However, my step **paused** as I bit into the bread. It was super moist and fragrant. "This is probably the best cornbread I have ever had." I said to myself. Then I saw Paula silently arranging the cornbread on the plate. I went close to her and asked if she had brought it, she

44

said yes. "I – I added buttermilk. That's why it's so tasty." She said, shyly. In her introverted look, I found myself being drawn to her. It was like a surprise box, and I loved the feeling of being amazed. In her, I found potential.

　　我和寶拉是在各家帶菜的家庭派對上認識的。她並不出眾：沒有驚為天人的美貌、沒有出奇的智慧或幽默感，總而言之就是普通。我在派對上大部分的時間都沒注意到她，因為，嗯，正常的男性都會想跟漂亮有魅力的女性聊天吧？所以在我跟幾個女孩聊天後，我回到飯廳去拿點心。在放著吐司小點和蝦子酒杯的桌上，我發現了玉米麵包。隨手抓了一個後，我轉身回到裡面的房間。

　　然而，就在我咬下玉米麵包的同時，我停下腳步；玉米麵包濕潤且香氣四溢。「我想這是我吃過最好吃的玉米麵包耶。」我心想。接著我發現寶拉默默擺放著桌上的玉米麵包。我走過去問這是否是她帶來的，她給我肯定的答案。「我加了發酵奶，這就是好吃的秘訣。」她害羞地說。在她閃爍內斂的眼神裡，我發現自己被她吸引了。就像個驚喜箱一樣，我也喜歡被驚喜到的感覺。在她身上，我看見了這種可能性。

◉ Cornbread

Since the country of America was discovered and later filled with European immigrants, corn has remained the main food resource for many local residents. Nowadays, on a typical American dining table, cornbread is still common. It is usually made of cornmeal, a coarsely ground corn, and baking powder. It can be baked in the oven or cooked stovetop in a skillet. Although one can always make the cornbread plain and enjoy it with butter, savory cornbread is also desirable. Cheddar cheese, bacon or jalapeño are good elements to make cornbread more enjoyable.

◉ 玉米麵包

美洲是在被歐洲人發現後，才有移民來定居，因此對許多當地人而言，時至今日，玉米仍擔任大部分食物來源。今天，玉米麵包在美國的餐桌上仍十分常見。玉米麵包主要由粗磨而成的玉米和泡打粉製成，可以用烤箱烤，也可以在爐子上用鍋子烤熟。雖然原味的玉米麵包抹奶油就很好吃，但鹹味的玉米麵包更引人垂涎。切達起司、培根和墨西哥辣椒都是讓玉米麵包更美味的元素。

字彙補充包

potluck n 每人帶一道菜的聚餐	stunningly　adv 令人驚艷地
unexpectedly adv 出乎意料地	humorous　adj 幽默的
ordinary　adj 平庸的	for the better part of 大部分時間的
tend to　傾向於	aside from　除了…
spot　v 發現	pause　v 暫停
introverted　adj 內斂的	potential　n 可能性
be filled with　充滿…	immigrant　n 移民
resource　n 資源	nowadays　adv 現今
coarsely　adv 粗略地	stovetop　n 爐灶
desirable　adj 合意的	element　n 元素

Nachos
焗烤玉米片

 情緣園地 MP3 10

Cooking is not only a woman's thing; actually, it is a man's thing. How can a **delicate** little woman **handle** a pot of grilled juicy **tenderloin**, or flip a whole pizza dough overhead? This almost makes me laugh, ha! That **smoking-hot** Latin babe just told me that she had no interest in **dudes** that don't take a step in the kitchen, but she will see what I've got.

Tortilla chips, I prefer blue; chopped onions, chopped tomatoes, **ground** beef, chili, cumin, coriander, plus a big pile of shredded cheese. **That's what I'm talking about.** Don't wait babe, dig in! Green jalapeño sauce right here, I bet you will never **have enough**. Look at those eyes, aren't they amazing? Now she's **hooked on** me. I knew it. This is **addictive** baby; I don't blame you. The recipe?

Hmm, maybe after a few cups of tequila sunrise. What do you say?

下廚不是女性的專利；說實話，這其實是件相當陽剛的事。一位纖細的小姐怎麼能抬起一整鍋炙燒多汁的梅花豬肉，或把披薩麵團舉到頭上旋轉？天大的笑話，哈！那位火辣的拉丁妞剛告訴我，她對不進廚房的老兄沒興趣，她很快就會見識到我的能耐了。

我偏愛藍玉米製成的脆片，洋蔥丁、番茄丁、牛絞肉、辣椒粉、茴香子、香菜、最後是像山一樣高的起士絲。這才像話。寶貝，別等了，開吃吧！青辣椒醬在這，我保證妳會欲罷不能。看看那陶醉的眼神，銷魂的美味，對吧？現在她對我有興趣了，就說吧。這令人上癮，寶貝，我不怪妳。妳想知道食譜？嗯，先來幾杯龍舌蘭日出，妳看怎樣？

美食重點介紹

● Nachos

Originated in Mexico, Nachos are now a popular bar food all-over America. The method of making nachos **varies** from chef to chef; there is no must-put in the recipe. Usually, onions, tomatoes and chili are the basic ingredients, on a **layer** of tortilla chips. Other than that, ground beef, **sunny eggs** or other vegetables can also be applied. To **finish up**, a thick layer of shredded cheese is necessary. Sharp cheddar is often used, as it is probably the most popular cheese **topping** for all kinds of pub food. Nachos can be eaten by spoon or by hand. One can be **feasting on** nachos with one hand and holding a **craft** beer in the other.

● 焗烤玉米片

源起於墨西哥，焗烤玉米片現在是風靡全美的酒吧必點菜。作法依廚師而有不同，沒有固定的食譜。基本上，洋蔥、番茄和辣椒是固定班底，底層是墨西哥玉米片。除此之外，牛絞肉、半熟蛋和其他蔬菜也可以入菜。完成料理的最後步驟，是撒上一層厚厚的起士絲。銳利切達起士很常見，幾乎在每樣酒吧料理裡都見得到它的蹤跡。焗烤玉米片可以用手或湯匙食用，你可以一邊抓食玉米片，一邊手握精釀啤酒開懷暢飲。

字彙補充包

delicate　adj 纖細的	handle　v 處理
tenderloin　n 豬里肌	smoking-hot adj 火辣的（人或物）
dude　n 老兄；小子	ground　adj 絞碎的
that's what I'm talking about 這才像話	have enough　欲罷不能
hook on　對⋯著迷	addictive　adj 令人上癮的
originated　起源自	vary　v 相異
layer　n 層	sunny egg　n 荷包蛋
finish up　結尾	topping　n 放在最上層的配料
feast on　大快朵頤	craft　n 手藝

Chili
辣豆燉肉

 情緣園地 MP3 *11*

My car has just been **towed**. I lost one **client** in the morning, **was unable to** finish my papers in the afternoon, and now my car's gone. Today is definitely **not my day**. It's good to be home anyway. Jessica would be mad if she knew what happened to me. Hm, I smell the **aroma** of chili. Chili is my favorite.

Jessica is a very **understanding** woman; we started to live together about one year ago. She is caring, organized and calm. Sometimes I **wonder** why she is willing to stay with a less successful lawyer like me. This chili is good. The beef is **tender**, the black beans are soft, and the **broth** is slightly tangy and flavorful. This is the way I like it. I tell Jessica how **dumb** I was today, hoping she won't be upset. To my surprise, she just refills my bowl with chili and says, "Everything is gonna be alright."

　　我的車被拖吊了。早上我失去了一個客戶，下午沒把該完成的文件完成，現在車子又被拖。衰到家了。總而言之，能回家真好。潔西卡要是知道我幹的好事，她一定會很生氣。嗯，我聞到辣豆燉肉的味道了，那是我的最愛。

　　潔西卡是個相當善解人意的女人，我們大約一年前開始住在一起。她很體貼、嚴謹且溫和，有時候我會納悶她怎麼甘願跟我這個不怎麼成功的律師在一起。辣豆燉肉真好吃，牛肉軟嫩，黑豆熟爛，湯微酸且充滿鮮味，我就愛這一味。我告訴潔西卡今天我幹的蠢事，暗自希望她不會發怒。出乎意料的，她默默的幫我盛滿另一碗辣豆燉肉，並告訴我：「一切都會沒事的」。

● Chili

A Mexican stew that serves as a main dish. The **major** ingredients are ground beef, black beans, tomatoes, and beef stock. Beef is **sautéed** with onion to start, giving the whole soup a meaty taste. Then, beans, tomatoes, and other ingredients are added with stock to cook for a long time, in order to bring the flavors together. Chili is a perfect meal on a winter night. With family **gathered** around the table, the aroma is in the air and the taste is just heart-warming. Garlic bread, **toasted** rye bread or just a plain sliced **loaf** would pair up nicely with this **splendid yumminess**.

● 辣豆燉肉

這是一道作為主食上桌的墨西哥湯品。主要原料有牛絞肉、黑豆、番茄和牛高湯。牛肉先和洋蔥爆炒，這會在湯中增添肉的香味。黑豆、番茄和其他食材與牛高湯一起加入燉煮許久，好讓所有滋味完全釋放。辣豆燉肉非常適合冬日晚餐。家人聚集在桌邊，香氣在空中飄散，滋味則從口裡暖到心裡。大蒜麵包、烤黑麥麵包或原味吐司都很適合與這道菜一同享用。

字彙補充包

tow　ⓥ 拖吊	be unable to 無法…；不能…
client　ⓝ 顧客；客戶	aroma　ⓝ 香味；香氣
today is not my day 諸事不順、走霉運	wonder　ⓥ 納悶；懷疑
understanding　adj 體貼的	broth　ⓝ 高湯
tender　adj 柔軟的	major　adj 主要的
dumb　adj 蠢的；笨的	gather　ⓥ 聚集
sauté　ⓥ 炒、煎	rye　ⓝ 裸麥、黑麥
toast　ⓥ 烤	yumminess　ⓝ 美味；美食
splendid　adj 很棒的、璀璨的	

Tortilla Chips
墨西哥玉米片

 MP3 *12*

The encounter with Peter on my trip to New Mexico is like tortilla chips and salsa. We just **can't help but** finish the whole **package** of chips once opened. Guacamole is also a good **companion** for tortilla chips, but for some reason, the mildness **turns us off**.

The south is **vast**, hot and dry. Sometimes I feel the heat is going to **defeat** me, but every time the **stimulation** of tortilla chips and salsa keeps me going. I ask Peter why he likes me, he just laughs and points to the sky. "Do you ever wonder why a cactus can survive in the desert?" he asks, one hand dipping a chip in salsa and eating it. "It's made that way." It's **true that** things in life can't always be explained, so why not enjoy the moment while we are alive?

　　在新墨西哥旅行時與彼得的邂逅就像墨西哥玉米片和莎莎醬。我們都喜歡辣味的莎莎醬，那跟墨西哥玉米片最對味，每次開一包脆片就吃到見底。酪梨醬也跟墨西哥玉米片合拍，但不知為何，那股溫吞的感覺沒辦法勾起我們的食慾。

　　南方地廣，天氣又熱又乾。有時候我覺得炎熱簡直要把我擊垮了，但每次墨西哥玉米片和莎莎醬的刺激總能拉我一把，讓我繼續旅行。我問彼得喜歡我哪一點，他大笑著指向天空說：「你想過為什麼仙人掌能在沙漠中生存嗎？」他邊問，邊一手將玉米片蘸到莎莎醬裡並一口吃掉。「因為天生如此。」的確，生命中不是每件事都能得到解釋，那何不在活著的時候及時行樂呢？

◉ Tortilla Chips

Although these fried, sometimes baked crispy corn chips are popular in the States from coast to coast, in Asia they are mostly recognized as the brand "Doritos". Flavored chips are fancy and exciting, but unseasoned tortilla chips pair up perfectly with salsa and guacamole (an avocado dip). In restaurants, chips and dip serve as a good appetizer. It can also be served as a slightly more complicated yet tempting dish: nachos. Yellow corn tortilla chips are the most common, but white corn and blue corn are also available. Just like potato chips, tortilla chips are an all-time classic that stands the test of time.

◉ 墨西哥玉米片

雖然這道油炸或烘烤而成的脆餅在全美十分普及，在亞洲，大部分人的印象卻僅止於多力多滋。調味玉米片的確酷炫又刺激，但未調味的玉米片才能和莎莎醬及酪梨醬完美合拍。玉米片和沾醬在餐廳是一道美味的開胃菜，也可將其製成更複雜且更引人食慾的焗烤玉米片。黃玉米片最常見，但白玉米和藍玉米一樣可以製成玉米片。就像洋芋片一樣，墨西哥玉米片也是經得起時間考驗的經典。

字彙補充包

can't help but
無法克制做某事

package　n 包裹；一包

companion　n 伴侶；夥伴

turn sb.off　使某人喪失興致

vast　adj 遼闊的

defeat　v 打敗；打倒

stimulation　n 刺激

true that　的確…

from coast to coast
全國；境內

recognize　v 認出；辨識

fancy　adj 奇幻的；酷炫的

pair up with　與…搭配

appetizer　n 開胃菜

complicated　adj 複雜的

tempting　adj 誘人的

available　adj 可取得的

all-time　adj 長久的

stand the test of
經得起…的考驗

unit 13

Falafel
中東蔬菜球

 情緣園地　 MP3 *13*

Mandy started her maple syrup stand not long after I **joined** Farmer's market. Since then, I had been trying to have a friendship with her, but what I had gotten were nothing but some polite yet **conservative** dialogues.

She didn't speak much, but her smile melted me every time. With a **bunch** of spinach in hand, I walked toward her and asked if she'd like to have a **trade**. She smiled, quietly turned around and grabbed a Ziploc bag from her **cooler**; to my surprise, it was falafel. We sat down and she started to share her **background** of being an **immigrant** from the mid-east. The falafel, **crunchy** outside and soft inside, was full of flavor. Then it hit me that it was just like Mandy – quiet outwardly but **passionate** inwardly. As she spoke, her eyes **sparkled** and got all **vibrant**. At that moment, I knew that we would become close friends, or more than just friends.

曼蒂是在我加入這個農夫市集不久後開設她的楓糖漿攤位的，從那時開始，我就一直試著要跟她做朋友，但目前為止，我們的關係僅止於相敬如賓的談話。

她話不多，但她的微笑每次都叫我融化。我拿了一把菠菜走向她，並問她想不想以物易物。她安靜地笑了笑，轉身拿出一個密封袋，竟是中東蔬菜球。我們並肩坐下，她開始說起她身為中東移民的背景。蔬菜球外皮酥脆，內餡軟糯，滋味深遠。我突然發現這就像曼蒂——外表冷淡，內心火熱。當她說話時，她的雙眼發亮且生氣昂揚。那時我便確信我們將成為摯友，甚至不僅僅是朋友。

● Falafel

A deep-fried crispy ball made of chickpea and spices. Usually considered to have its origins in Egypt, falafel is well-spread all over Europe and America, and it's popular especially in the middle-east. It is a **vegetarian**-friendly food and it's served **commonly** on the street, hot. It can be **stuffed** in a pita bread, **along with** tomato, cucumber and lettuce to make it into a sandwich, as well as with dipping sauce as an **appetizer** in restaurants. One can also **pan-fry** the falafels to get a less **greasy** version, but it is at its best when deep-fried properly. The best companion with falafel is baba ganoush, a roasted eggplant purée.

● 中東蔬菜球

這是一種由鷹嘴豆和香料油炸而成的蔬菜球，通常被認為起源自埃及。中東蔬菜球在歐洲及美洲都得見其蹤跡，特別在中東十分受到歡迎。這是一款素食小吃，經常在街頭上販售並以熱食型態供應。中東蔬菜球可以作為口袋麵包的配料，搭配番茄、小黃瓜和萵苣，便成了三明治；也可以搭配沾醬，在餐廳是一道開胃菜。中東蔬菜球也可以用煎的，是較少油的健康版本，但油炸會帶出最佳美味。中東蔬菜球的最佳拍檔是一種將烤過的茄子打碎的茄子糊沾醬。

字彙補充包

join ⓥ 加入	conservative adj 內斂、保守的
bunch ⓝ 捆、束	trade ⓝ 交易
cooler ⓝ 保冰箱	background ⓝ 家庭背景
immigrant ⓝ 移民	crunchy adj 酥脆的
passionate adj 熱情的	sparkle ⓥ 發亮
vibrant adj 生氣蓬勃的	vegetarian ⓝ 素食主義者
commonly adv 常見	stuffed adj 填充的
along with 一同	appetizer ⓝ 開胃菜
pan-fry adj 油煎的	greasy adj 油膩的

Pani Puri
炸脆餅小點

 情緣園地 MP3 *14*

The bustling Bombay produces awesome people like James. We work for the same newspaper, and we always **dine in** good restaurants. It seems that the dirty and the **livestock**-friendly streets **have nothing to do with** us.

Until one day James takes me for a "special treat". He says it's his favorite food since childhood, and he takes me to a **filthy** vendor on a **muddy** road. He can't be serious, I say to myself, as I watch the vendor **pouring** some green water **over** fried puffy pastry shells stuffed with God knows what. Ew, I don't even want to get close to it. James takes up a puff and hands me another. "Cheers!" He says with a smile on his face. I make up my mind and bite into it – and the pastry cracks and **releases** the flavor, like a delicious Indian rainbow in my mouth.

　　雜沓的孟買市產生了像是James這樣的優秀人才。我們在同家新聞社上班，且常到不錯的餐廳約會。感覺上，塵土飛揚、動物橫行的街道好像跟我們毫無關係。

　　直到有一天，詹姆斯帶我去「特別獎勵」。他說那是他從兒時起最愛的食物，結果竟是一個位在泥濘街上的骯髒小販。他不是認真的吧，我心想，邊看著小販老闆把某種綠色的液體潑到裡面塞了鬼才知道是什麼的炸球餅裡面。噁，我完全不想靠近。詹姆斯拿起一個炸球餅，並遞給我另一個。「乾杯！」他微笑著說。我硬著頭皮一口咬下去，霎時，豐富的滋味在嘴裡碎裂開來，像一道印度七色彩虹。

◉ Pani puri

A common street food throughout India and the surrounding countries. "Pani" literally means water. Here, it indicates a light sauce made of several herbs and spices. Its color can be green or red, depending on the ingredients. "Puri" refers to deep-fried pastry puffs that are hollow inside. When served, puris are pressed down in the middle, stuffed with a potato-pureé based stuffing, and finished with drizzles of "pani". In India, the puris are piled up on the vendors' little cart. Customers come and eat on the spot, then they just dump the trash on the ground. It is believed that the best pani puri can only be found on the street.

◉ 炸脆餅小點

這是一種在印度及其周邊國家相當常見的街頭小吃。「pani」意思是水,在這裡意指一種由多種香草及香料組成的沾醬。其顏色可綠可紅,視成分而定。「puri」是一種中空的油炸麵糰,通常要吃的時候,會從中心壓下去弄個小洞,塞入以馬鈴薯泥為主組成的餡料,並淋上沾醬作結。在印度,炸好的麵糰在攤販上堆成小山,客人買了當場吃,並在吃完後把垃圾隨地丟棄。一般認為最好吃的炸脆餅得要在街頭上才找得到。

字彙補充包

get used to　習慣於…	bustling　adj 忙碌的
dine in　在…用餐	livestock　n 牲口
have nothing to do with 跟…沒關係	filthy　adj 骯髒的
muddy　adj 泥濘的	pour sth. over sth. 把…倒到…之上
release　v 釋放	surrounding　adj 周遭的
literally　adv 字面上地	indicate　v 意謂
herb　n 香草	depend on　依靠；依…而定
refer to　意即…	hollow　adj 中空的
drizzle　v 淋（少許液體）	pile up　把…堆疊得很高
on the spot　當場；現場	dump　v 丟棄；傾倒（垃圾）

unit 15

Biriyani
香料炒飯

 情緣園地 MP3 *15*

As I see the pile of rice arriving, Joshua starts to scoop the chili-colored rice into his mouth. The next thing I know is definitely not the way of eating it, but the burst of spices flavor on my tongue, like a spicy bomb.

It even keeps **stinging** after I **swallow**. "The water won't help, and we enjoy that.", Joshua says, with a **casual** expression on his face. He **reclines** at the table, with one hand throwing over-spiced fried rice into his mouth **unceasingly**. How could any human **alive** on earth **tolerate** this? This chicken biriyani is certainly too spicy! Yet the man sitting in front of me enjoying this food makes my heart beat. Not until today did I get to know the true spiciness of India – Chinese, Korean or even Malaysian ain't **comparable**, because I have fallen in love with this handsome fire-breather.

當我看到那堆如山高的炒飯上桌時，約書亞便開始將嫣紅色的炒飯舀進嘴裡。接下來我只知道，不是吃的方式而是香料味道在舌尖爆開，像辣椒炸彈。

甚至在我嚥下之後，舌尖還感到陣陣刺痛。喝水也沒用，我們就愛這一味，約書亞說。他輕鬆隨意的倚在桌邊，一隻手不間斷地將超辣的炒飯丟進嘴裡。世上怎麼有活人可以忍受這個啊？這道印度炒飯明顯是太辣了！但這位坐在我對面，享受著佳餚的男士卻讓我心跳加速。直到今天我才知道印度真正的辛辣，中國、韓國甚至馬來西亞的辣度都無法與之匹敵，因為我已經愛上了這位火辣達令。

● Biriyani

Like most Indian dishes, biriyani is composed of basmati rice cooked with many different spices. The central spice is garam masala, a mix of spices tailored for Indian dishes which creates a unique flavor. If using meat, the meat has to be marinated in a mix of spices first, which usually includes fresh coriander leaves, mint leaves and green chili. Beef, chicken, mutton or shrimp are usually added to Biriyani. Many people enjoy vegetarian versions, too. Sometimes there are egg halves along with onion yogurt on the side. It can be served plain, but for most of the Indians, serving it up spicy will be more appealing.

● 香料炒飯

就如同大多數的印度菜一樣,香料炒飯使用相當多的香料;而在眾多的香料中,馬薩拉尤其不可或缺。馬薩拉是由數種香料混合而成、印度獨有的香料,能為印度料理製造特有的風味。若使用肉類,需先將肉在數種香料中醃過,包括新鮮的香菜、薄荷葉和青辣椒。牛肉、雞肉、羊肉和蝦類常見於此道料理,有時水煮蛋與洋蔥優格會一起上桌。香料炒飯可以做成不辣版本,但是對多數印度人來說,還是要辣一點才夠味。

字彙補充包

pile　**n** 堆、疊	freeze　**v** 結凍
scoop　**v** 用湯匙舀	keep up　跟進
awkwardly　**adv** 笨拙地	burst　**v** 爆發
sting　**v** 刺、螫	swallow　**v** 吞嚥
casual　**adj** 隨意的	recline　**v** 斜倚
unceasingly　**adv** 不停地	alive　**adj** 活的
tolerate　**v** 忍受	comparable　**adj** 可匹敵的
be composed of　由…組成	tailor for　為…量身打造
unique　**adj** 獨一無二的	marinate　**v** 醃漬
on the side　作為配菜、配料	appealing　**adj** 吸引人的

Part **1**
美食異國情緣篇

Part **2**
美食口語強化篇

Green Papaya Salad
青木瓜沙拉

 情緣園地 MP3 ▶ 16

The crushed crab in our salad made Dan and I scared. Language barriers in Thailand mattered.

Dan and I met in the **hostel** the first night I arrived in Bangkok. He was funny and bold. After a little chat, we soon decided to **explore** Thailand together. However, our biggest **crises** happened the very next day: this dish of green papaya salad in front of us. I could still see the uncrushed leg of crab with its **fur** on it. Was it raw or cooked? We had no **clue**. Yet, to my surprise, Dan moved **forward** and took a bite. "If I'm **poisoned**, at least I saved your life." He joked. I **observed** his face, **anxiously** wondering if he would survive. "It's good!" Dan finally said, and I was relieved. Dan has become my travel **companion** since, and after our adventure, we moved back to my hometown together.

　　我們沙拉中搗碎的螃蟹使我和丹飽受驚嚇。在泰國這裡語言障礙真的有影響。

　　丹和我是在我抵達曼谷的第一晚，在青年旅社認識的。他既風趣又勇敢，我們稍微聊了一會後，便決定要一起探索泰國。然而，巨大的危機第二天就發生了，也就是我們面前這盤青木瓜沙拉。我還看得到一隻沒被搗碎的蟹腳耶，蟹腳上還有毛。這是生的還是熟的啊？我們沒有半點頭緒。然而，丹卻出乎意料的決定率先動筷。「如果我被毒死了，至少我還救了妳一命。」他開玩笑的說。我觀察著他的臉，心急如焚的想知道他是否沒事。「好吃耶！」終於丹開口這麼說，我也鬆了一口氣。丹從那時起就成了我的旅伴，而旅程結束後，我們便一起回到我的家鄉定居了。

● Green Papaya Salad

This is an **iconic** salad for Thailand. The combination of green papaya salad is unlimited. For the base, fish sauce, coconut sugar, lemon juice, garlic paste and red pepper are **critical**. The sauce is sour-sweet, sometimes hot according to taste. Green papaya is peeled, deseeded and shredded. Usually, it is soaked in ice water for crispiness. Tomatoes and fried peanuts are there for a little bit of tanginess and crunchiness. As for protein, seafood is the mainstream, but not the only option. It **ranges** from crab, shrimp, to fish and preserved egg.

● 青木瓜沙拉

這是一道泰國指標性的沙拉，其組合有無限多種可能。以基底來說，魚露、椰糖、檸檬汁、蒜頭和朝天椒是必須的。醬汁又酸又甜，根據個人的口味也可以做得相當辣。青木瓜需先削皮、去籽並切絲，之後浸泡於冰水中以保爽脆。番茄和炸花生為這道菜帶來一絲酸味和酥脆感。至於添加的肉類，海鮮是主流，但並非只能加海鮮。螃蟹、蝦、魚類和鹹蛋都可見於此道菜中。

字彙補充包

astonish **v** 驚訝；詫異	crush **v** 壓碎；擊垮
horrified **adj** 嚇壞的	frighten **v** 嚇唬；恐懼
tourist **n** 觀光客	barrier **n** 障礙；藩籬
fatal **adj** 致命的	hostel **n** 青年旅館
explore **v** 探索	crises **n** 危機
fur **n** 毛	clue **n** 線索
forward **adv** 向前；在前	poison **v** 下毒
observe **v** 觀察	anxiously **adv** 焦慮地
companion **n** 伴侶	iconic **adj** 指標性的
critical **adj** 重要的	range **n** 範圍

Part**1**
美食異國情緣篇

Part**2**
美食口語強化篇

unit 17

Pineapple Bun with Butter
冰火菠蘿油

Who can **reject** butter, ever? But for my own good and to **keep in shape**, I eat it very **moderately**. When I see people on the street biting and **savoring** their pineapple bun with butter, I'm like "wow...", especially when it is Gina. She eats **like no one else**. For her, there is no **concern** about calories in this **universe**, yet she is amazingly in shape and beautiful.

When I look at her, and see the shiny butter and **grease** that **sticks** to her lips and sometimes her cheek, I say to myself, she is the one for me. I started going out with her, and most of the time, we go to the pineapple bun **vendor**. Seriously, with a bun like this and Yuanyang **in hand**, who can ask for more?

　　誰能抗拒奶油的魅力呢？但為了我的健康和身材著想，我很克制。當我看到人們當街大啖冰火菠蘿油時，我常不禁發出「哇…」的感嘆，尤其是吉娜。她品嘗美食的模樣獨樹一幟。對她來說，卡路里這東西好像不存在似的，但她卻保有極佳的身材及容貌。

　　當我看著她，她嘴角因奶油閃閃發亮，有時臉頰上也沾到少許，我就決定她是我要的女孩。我開始跟她出雙入對，大部分時間，我們會光顧冰火菠蘿油的小販。說真的，有美食在手，配上一杯鴛鴦奶茶，夫復何求？

Part **1**
美食異國情緣篇

Part **2**
美食口語強化篇

 **美食重點介紹**

● Pineapple Bun with Butter

Pineapple Bun is a very common and casual food for Asian people. The crust on top of the bun **cracks** when it's baked, **thus resembling** a pineapple. However, there is no pineapple in the bun. In Taiwan, the crust is usually **plain** or chocolate flavor, and sometimes the bun is stuffed with pork floss. In Hong Kong, the bun is stuffed with a thick frozen piece of butter. The Bun will be **heated up** to **complement** the frozen butter, in order to create a hot 'n cold tasting experience. In Japan, the bun is cut in half and served with cabbage, ham and cheese as a sandwich.

● 冰火菠蘿油

菠蘿麵包對亞洲人來說是相當常見且隨意的小食。麵包上面有層奶酥，烤好的時候會裂開，看起來像菠蘿（鳳梨）；然而麵包體中並無菠蘿成分。在台灣，常見原味或巧克力味的奶酥頂，有時候麵包裡會塞肉鬆。在香港，麵包切半並放入一塊厚厚的冷凍奶油。麵包會事先熱過，再配上冰凍的奶油而產生冰火交融的口感。在日本，麵包切半並夾進生菜、火腿和起司作為三明治享用。

字彙補充包

a fan of　喜歡某事	reject　**v** 拒絕
keep in shape　保持身材	moderately　**adv** 適度地
savor　**v** 品嘗	like no one else　有自己的風格
concern　**v** 在意	universe　**n** 宇宙
grease　**n** 油脂	vendor　**n** 小販
in hand　手握…	crack　**v** 裂開
thus　因此	resemble　**v** 與…相似
plain　**n** 原味	heat up　加熱
complement　**v** 與…相配	stick　**v** 黏、貼

Part **1** 美食異國情緣篇

Part **2** 美食口語強化篇

Oden
關東煮

 情緣園地 MP3 ▸ 18

In Japan, convenience stores run 24/7. It is super easy to get a snack or drink in the **dead of night**, especially when it is in walking **distance**. I love fish balls and cabbage rolls, **whereas** Kaori likes daikon and mushrooms.

We meet at a 7-11 on the corner of the street, and soon two bowls of **steaming** hot oden **packed** soup are in our hands. "Don't you feel that the colder the weather is, the tastier oden will be?", she asked with a mushroom in her mouth. I bite into a fish ball, and the juice comes out to fill my mouth. **I couldn't agree with her more**. Holding a bowl of soup like this is as **comfy** as lying under a fluffy blanket. **In truth** having Kaori here is what makes the Oden truly enjoyable.

　　在日本，便利商店是 24 小時營業的，全年無休。要在大半夜買個零食或飲料超方便，尤其是走路就會到。我喜歡魚丸和高麗菜卷，香織則是白蘿蔔和香菇的愛好者。

　　我們在街角的 7-11 碰面，很快的，我們手裡便各自捧著一碗裝滿關東煮的熱湯。「你不覺得天氣越冷，關東煮似乎越美味嗎？」她邊嚼著香菇邊問道。我大口咬下魚丸，湯汁霎時充滿在口中。她說得對極了，像這樣捧著一碗湯就像窩在軟綿綿的被窩裡一樣舒服。不過再怎麼說，香織還是讓這一切美味起來的決定性因素。

● Oden

Although the **recipe differs from** family to family, oden serves as an important role in winter **throughout** Japan. In Japanese families, having a pot of oden for dinner is **undoubtedly** the most **thrilling** thing for a winter day. Usually, the family gather together around a big pot, and the ingredients are added according to one's taste. Daikon, konbu kelp, kastuo and konyaku are commonly used as the **basis** for soup. As for oden itself, there is no **limit**. Some prefer the classic cabbage roll and deep fried fish cake, while others prefer **stewed** apple and black sesame tofu.

● 關東煮

雖然關東煮作法家家不同，但對日本人來說，關東煮在冬天至關重要。在一個日本家庭裡，一鍋熱呼呼的關東煮晚餐絕對是冬日裡最令人引頸企盼的事。通常全家會圍坐在一個大大的鍋子旁，並依照個人喜好加入食材。由白蘿蔔、昆布、柴魚片和蒟蒻熬煮的湯底相當普遍。至於關東煮的料是什麼，倒是沒有強硬規定。有的人喜歡經典的高麗菜捲和甜不辣，有的人則愛煮蘋果和芝麻豆腐。

字彙補充包

dead of night　大半夜	distance　🅝 距離
whereas　而…	steaming　🆎 冒著蒸氣的
packed　🆎 裝滿…的	can't agree with sb. more 非常同意某人
comfy　comfortable 的口語	in truth　的確；事實是
recipe　🅝 食譜；作法	differ from　與…相異
throughout　貫穿；穿透	undoubtedly　🆎 毫無疑問地
thrilling　🆎 令人興奮的	basis　🅝 基底；基礎
limit　🅝 限制	stew　🆅 燉煮
24/7　一週二十四小時營業	

Part 1 美食異國情緣篇

Part 2 美食口語強化篇

Tamagoyaki
玉子燒

 情緣園地 19

It is **odd** to have a sweet scrambled egg, isn't it? Actually, it's sweet yet salty. Whenever I bite into a juicy tamagoyaki, with its two **opposite** flavors dancing on top of my tongue so **harmoniously**, I can't help but close my eyes and think of my childhood.

Sumito likes my tamagoyaki a lot. It's not overly sweet, he **claims**, yet the **chunkiness** of sugar is in every bite, **along with** the aroma of soy sauce which is **brought out** by the salt. Sumito and I grew up in the same **neighborhood**.

We soon moved to a bigger city. Familiar taste and texture of tamagoyaki somehow eases our homesickness in the bustling urban environment. No matter how the world changes, we are not alone

　　甜煎蛋聽起來很怪，對吧？事實上，是既甜又鹹。每當我大口咬下多汁的玉子燒時，兩種相反的味道在舌尖完美融合並跳躍著，總讓我不禁閉上雙眼，並讓這股味道將我帶回到兒時。

　　純人很喜歡我做的玉子燒，他說不會太甜，但是每口都吃得到砂糖的脆脆顆粒，並嘗得到被鹽帶出的醬油香味。純人和我從小一起長大，我們上同一所小學、初中、高中。

　　我們很快就搬到城市生活。玉子燒那熟悉的滋味和外觀不知怎地一解我們的鄉愁。不論世界怎麼變，我們都不孤單。

● Tamagoyaki

A traditional dish that almost every Japanese family prepares differently. Each family has their **unique** way of making tamagoyaki, which always **reminds one** of home. Tamagoyaki, in Japanese, means "fried egg" or "scrambled egg". It is a **layered** fried egg that is **rolled** up, then cut into bite-size pieces. The **seasoning** includes sugar, salt, mirin and soy sauce. Tamagoyaki is considered sweeter in southern Japan than in the north. There is no rule for making tamagoyaki; herbs, cheese and mentaiko tamagoyaki are common **variations** in izakaya, Japanese traditional **bistros**.

◉ 玉子燒

這是一種傳統日本料理，幾乎每個家庭都有自己的製作方式。每個家庭依據自己獨一無二的食譜，製作出的玉子燒常能叫人嘗出懷念的家鄉味。玉子燒在日文意指「煎／炒蛋」，是一種層層相疊的煎蛋皮，捲起成柱狀並切成一口大小。調味料包括砂糖、鹽、味霖和醬油。南日本的玉子燒口味通常被認為比北日本甜。玉子燒沒有既定的製作方式，香草、起司和明太子玉子燒在日本居酒屋（日式傳統小酒館）相當常見。

字彙補充包

odd **adj** 奇怪的；怪異的	claim **v** 主張
harmoniously **adv** 和諧地	along with　與…一起
chunkiness **n** 酥脆感	neighborhood **n** 社區；社群
bring out　帶出	familiar **adj** 熟悉的
texture **n** 外型	unique **adj** 獨一無二的
remind sb.of 讓某人想起…	layered **adj** 層層疊疊的
roll **v** 捲起	seasoning **n** 調味
variation **n** 變化	bistro **n** 小酒館；小餐館
opposite **adj** 相反的	

Rice Cake
年糕

 *20*

I **treasure** the customs and **moral** values, which teach me to respect the **ancestors** and give thanks for every piece of food. Aida shares the same thought with me. For young people in our **generation**, this is definitely not common. Aida and I met in college. We were in the same student club. She and I **built up** our relationship gradually, **steadily**.

Now we are both working full-time, but **sparing** time to be with family and friends has been a big part of our lives. We both like azuki bean rice cake, fried or baked. Our grandparents are old enough to make the best rice cakes, and we enjoy them every year. The most important thing in life is the people one shares the moment with, and I am **more than** certain that our lives will **be** so involved in each other's. We will **stick to** each other like rice cake, and nothing can **break us apart**.

　　我很重視習俗和道德價值，例如尊重先祖、對每一份食物感懷在心等等。愛妲跟我有一樣的看法。對我們這一代的年輕人而言，要維持這樣的想法相當不容易。愛妲和我在大學的社團相識，我們的感情逐漸且穩定地培養茁壯。

　　現在我們都在工作了，但是花時間與家人、朋友相聚仍是我們生活中的一大部分。我們都很喜歡紅豆年糕，不管是炸的還是烤的。外公、外婆經驗老到，他們做的年糕是最棒的，而我們每年都享用到他們的手藝。人生中最重要的事情，莫過於那些與我們分享重要時刻的人們。我確信我們兩人的人生將彼此影響、深深糾結。就像年糕一樣，我們也「黏呼呼」在一塊兒了，沒有任何事能將我們分開。

● Rice Cake

Made with mashed rice and steamed afterward, rice cake has been a traditional food for new year throughout Korea, Japan and China for centuries. The ways of eating are much varied from country to country. In Taiwan, rice cake is usually slightly sweetened, pan-fried or deep-fried. In Japan, rice cake is cooked in soup with carrots, mushrooms and vegetables. The **paleness** of rice cake **floating** in the soup is a sign of good luck. Grilled rice cake with molasses is another common way rice cakes are served. In Korea, rice cake **is known for** Tteokbokki, which is a sauté-stew made with Korean hot sauce, along with onions, eggs and meat.

● 年糕

　　由搗爛的米蒸煮而成的年糕，是韓國、日本及中國好幾世紀以來的傳統年節料理。各國料理年糕的方式各異其趣。在台灣，年糕通常有點甜味，用煎炒或油炸的方式料理。在日本，年糕在湯裡和胡蘿蔔、香菇與蔬菜等一起做成雜煮，浮在湯裡的白年糕是好運的象徵。烤年糕佐黑糖蜜也是另一常見的料理方式。韓國以辣炒年糕聞名，這是一種將年糕與韓式辣醬、洋蔥、蛋和肉類一起炒熟的燉煮料理。

字彙補充包

treasure **v** 重視；珍視	moral **adj** 道德的
ancestor **n** 祖先	generation **n** 世代
build up　建立；培養	steadily **adv** 穩定地
spare **v** 省下；節約	more tha **n** ..　非常…
be involved in　牽扯在內	stick to　堅持做某事
break apart　使…分開	afterward **adv** 之後
century **n** 世紀	paleness **n** 蒼白
float **v** 浮（在水上）	be known for　因…有名

Part 1 美食異國情緣篇

Part 2 美食口語強化篇

Satay
沙嗲串燒

 情緣園地 MP3 *21*

How come girls are always waiting for guys' call? That's not **fair** at all. Oh! the doorbell rings…there you go! My darling is here! I can't believe this! I **get in** his car and there's another surprise: a gift box! Wow, that's my man… Luc took me to a nice restaurant, and ordered chicken satay.

"It'll be good." He **claimed**, with a confident smile. I **doubted** because I've never tried a chicken satay. There it comes, five flat chicken breast on the **skewers**, nice and **neat**. And there's a separate dish of satay sauce, which is dark brown and a little bit cloudy. I look up to Luc, **hesitantly**. Luc nods his head and tells me to **dig in**. **Undoubtedly**, everything's tasty. I've found a **prince charming** that not only knows how to surprise me, but also how to please my taste buds.

　　為什麼女孩們總是等待男生打電話來的那一方呢？這不公平啊。喔，門鈴響了…這不是我的達令嗎！我真不敢相信！上了車，那兒有另一個驚喜等著我：一個禮物盒！哇，不愧是我的男人。路克帶我到一間不錯的餐館，並點了雞肉沙嗲串。

　　這好吃。 他自信地笑著說。我挺懷疑的，因為我沒吃過雞肉沙嗲串。上菜了，五片串在烤肉串上的雞胸肉整齊又優雅的放在那兒；另一個盤子上放著沙嗲醬，顏色深棕且有點混濁。我遲疑地抬頭看著路克，他則點點頭示意我開動。無庸置疑的，食物棒呆了。我找到了一個白馬王子，他不只懂得製造驚喜，更知道怎麼取悅我的味蕾。

● Satay

Satay is an Indonesian dish, which much admired among Asian countries. Satay refers to both the meat and the sauce. Chicken, beef, pork or even tofu can be used as protein in this dish. The meat needs to be marinated first, then grilled on coals or wood until done. The morsels will be put piece after piece on a long stick and dipped into satay sauce. In Indonesia, this dish can be also high class or casual. It's in all star restaurant as well as on the street. Treating the guests with satay is a mark of hospitality in Malaysia.

● 沙嗲串燒

沙嗲串燒是一道印尼菜,在亞洲各國間相當有人氣。「沙嗲」一詞可用於指稱沙嗲串燒及沙嗲醬。雞、牛、豬或甚至豆腐都可用在這道菜上。肉先醃過之後,將其放在木炭或木材上烤熟。肉切成塊狀後串到長竹籤上,並沾沙嗲醬食用。在印尼,這道菜可高貴可平民;高級餐廳找得到,路邊小吃也有得買。在馬來西亞,招待客人吃沙嗲串是好客的象徵。

字彙補充包

get in　上車	claim　v 聲稱；説
doubt　v 懷疑；猜疑	skewer　n 烤肉串
neat　adj 整齊的	hesitantly　adv 猶疑地；遲疑地
dig in　開動	undoubtedly　adv 無庸置疑地
prince charming　白馬王子	please　v 取悦
taste buds　n 味蕾	admire　v 仰慕；喜歡
protein　n 蛋白質	marinate　v 醃漬
coal　n 木炭	morsel　n （食材）塊
casual　adj 隨意的	hospitality　n 好客
fair　adj 公平的	

unit
22

Century Egg and Tofu
皮蛋豆腐

 情緣園地 MP3 *22*

To be honest, I'm an IT nerd. Working in the IT industry for 2 years since graduation, I have to say this is the perfect job for me.

However, I **am** not **proud of** being a nerd. For instance, Judy – the **accountant** in the company, is such a **diva** for me. She is always neat and elegant, and I've been trying so hard to ask her out. This makes me **frustrated**. But hey! That's Judy! She actually has lunch in this noodle **stand** often as well, and she also orders century egg and tofu. Oh, I see her **reaching** in her pocket for coins⋯does she **happen to** be **short of** money for the moment? This is my chance! I'd love to share my century egg and tofu with her! Here she comes, looking **embarrassed**. This dish isn't expensive at all, but it's incredibly good, isn't it?

老實説，我的確是個科技宅男。自從大學畢業後，我已經在科技產業工作兩年了，這個工作對我來説很完美。

不過，我倒不以自己身為宅男為傲。比如説，茱蒂——我們公司的會計，是我的女神；她總是有條理又高雅，我一直很努力要約她出去，但沒能成功。這令我感到很挫敗。不過，嘿！那不是茱蒂嗎？她還滿常跟我在同一間麵攤吃午餐的，而且她也都會點皮蛋豆腐。喔，我看到她把手放在口袋裡掏錢了…是不是剛好沒帶夠錢啊？我的機會來了！我很樂意跟她分享皮蛋豆腐！她走過來了，看起來有點狼狽。這道小菜一點也不貴，但嘗起來可真美味，是吧？

● Century Egg and Tofu

Being known as thousands year egg or preserved egg, century egg is made by preserving duck eggs. It is black, half-transparent in the white, dark and gooey in the yolk. There are two main ways of making century egg and tofu: one, cut the silk tofu and half the egg. Place the egg on top and drizzle with soy sauce. Sprinkle some kastuo for garnish. The other: mix all those ingredients together and eat with a spoon. The second way may look messy, but the flavor is well-developed. As for tofu, instead of firm tofu, silk tofu is preferred, in order to achieve a smooth taste.

● 皮蛋豆腐

皮蛋也被稱為千年蛋或醃漬蛋,是一種加工後的鴨蛋。皮蛋是黑色的,蛋白呈半透明狀、蛋黃是流動的暗黑色。皮蛋豆腐有兩種主流吃法:一種是將嫩豆腐切塊,放上切片的皮蛋並淋上醬油,再撒上柴魚片做裝飾。第二種則是將上述材料全數攪拌混合,並用湯匙食用。第二種方式可能看起來髒兮兮的,但其味道倒是不錯。至於豆腐的選擇,嫩豆腐會比板豆腐好,吃起來才會有絹絲細滑的口感。

字彙補充包

be proud of　以…為榮	accountant　n 會計師
diva　n 女神	frustrated　adj 受挫的；挫敗的
stand　n 小吃攤；小攤販	reach　v 伸手；達到
happen to　剛好	short of　少了…
embarrassed　adj 尷尬的	incredibly　adv 難以置信地
preserve　v 封存；保存	transparent　adj 透明的
half　v 切成兩半	sprinkle　v 撒（一點點）
messy　adj 亂糟糟的	as for　至於
prefer　v 偏好	achieve　v 達成；實現

Part 1　美食異國情緣篇

Part 2　美食口語強化篇

unit 23

Daikon Cake

蘿蔔糕

Roaring scooters make the foreigner like Peter a little bit lost. I'd say that if you grow up in the **jungle**, you'll know how to **get along with** the beasts. I lead Peter into a traditional breakfast shop. "It's **shabby**, kind of." He frowns, following my step **reluctantly**.

Don't judge a book by its cover is my **motto**, and I think it's time for Peter to learn it. Hot, crispy daikon cake is my favorite breakfast. Peter tastes his first bite carefully, but soon his eyes **shine forth** and he starts to **devour** the cake.

"You surely **have a taste for** food." Peter **acclaims**, cheerfully savoring the daikon cake like it was a lobster. Once you enter the jungle, never think of leaving without a scratch. Now, Peter is absolutely in my trap; he is my prey.

　　呼嘯的摩托車讓像是彼得這樣的外國人有點迷失。彼得問。這個嘛，我會說若你在叢林長大，你總得學著跟野獸相處。我帶彼得到一家傳統早餐店，「有點髒。」他皺眉，不情願地跟上我的腳步。

　　不要以貌取人是我的座右銘，我想是讓彼得學習這句話的時候了。熱呼呼、硬脆的蘿蔔糕是我最愛的早餐。彼得小心翼翼地咬下第一口，突然眼睛一亮，並開始狼吞虎嚥的吃掉蘿蔔糕。

　　「你對食物很有品味嘛。」彼得讚美道，歡欣鼓舞的樣子好似眼前的蘿蔔糕是條龍蝦。一旦進了叢林，就別妄想毫髮無傷地離開。現在，彼得毫無疑問已掉入我的陷阱了；他是我的獵物。

◉ Daikon Cake

Daikon cake is a traditional Asian snack. Like its name, the main ingredient is shredded daikon. For the thickness of this cake, rice flour is added. Shrimp skin, fried onions and shredded scallops are necessary in traditional recipes, but there are vegetarian variations too. Daikon cake can be **steamed** or fried. The steamed daikon cake is tender and clean, whereas the fried one is crispy and **aromatic**. There is also a **similar** dish called taro cake, which **substitutes** daikon **with** taro. Daikon cake is also a snack in Hong Kong. Usually it is served at afternoon tea time along with other snacks such as steamed buns or dim sum.

◉ 蘿蔔糕

蘿蔔糕是一種傳統亞洲小吃。正如其名，蘿蔔糕的主要材料是刨成絲的白蘿蔔。為使蘿蔔糕成形，還會加入在來米粉。蝦皮、炒洋蔥和瑤柱在傳統蘿蔔糕食譜中是必要的材料，但也有素食的版本。蘿蔔糕可以蒸煮或油煎。蒸煮的蘿蔔糕軟綿又晶瑩剔透，油煎的蘿蔔糕則硬脆有香氣。另一小吃芋頭糕做法類似，僅是將蘿蔔替換成芋頭。蘿蔔糕在香港也是點心，經常會在下午茶時間與包子、燒賣等茶點一起供應。

Part **1**
美食異國情緣篇

字彙補充包

get along with　與…相處	jungle　[n] 熱帶叢林
reluctantly　[adj] 不情願的	shabby　[adj] 簡陋的
shine forth　閃亮；亮起	motto　[n] 格言；座右銘
have a taste for 對…有品味	devour　[v] 吞噬；狼吞虎嚥
scratch　[n] 擦傷；刮痕	acclaim　[v] 讚美；讚嘆
steam　[v] 蒸煮	prey　[n] 獵物
similar　[adj] 相似的	aromatic　[adj] 香氛的；有香氣的
roar　[v] 呼嘯；嚎叫	substitute A with B 以 B 取代 A

Part **2**
美食口語強化篇

103

Beef Tartare
韃靼牛肉

The egg, with its cooked white and **raw** yolk, looks so **enticing**. It sits on a bed of beef tartare, **garnished** with a **stem** of scallion. I **peep at** Thomas cute and charming, wondering what his next move will be.

Given how my last relationship ended, I'm taking it slow. Girls, if you want to **elevate** your value, don't be cheap. I want a guy that is not **careless** or impatient, so from the way they eat I will take a **glimpse** into who they are.

He moves away the scallion stem, and carefully cuts into the yolk. Look at the liquid **dripping** over the tartare! It looks so yummy. I take up the knife to cut mine, but just as the **blade** touches the yolk, it suddenly **splashes** out!

Thomas looks stunned for a second, but we both burst out laughing together immediately. Maybe from now on I can show more sincerity.

蛋白熟透、蛋黃卻還生生的雞蛋看起來引人食慾。生蛋穩坐在牛肉上，並以一條細蔥裝飾。我偷瞄了下湯瑪斯，帥又迷人，想知道他下一步會怎麼做。

考量到前段感情是如何結束的，我決定慢慢來。女孩們，如果妳們想提升自我價值的話，千萬不要太好追！我想要一個又細心又有耐心的男友，而從男孩們吃東西的樣子，我能對此人的個性略窺一二。

湯瑪斯拿開細蔥，並小心的切開蛋黃。瞧瞧那流淌而下的蛋汁！看起來真美味。我拿起餐刀準備切我的蛋，但就在刀鋒碰到蛋黃的那一刻，蛋汁突然噴射而出！湯瑪斯愣了一秒，接著我們兩個開始爆笑起來。唉，看來我是可以開始秀出我的真心了。

● Beef Tartare

Composed of lightly seasoned onion and raw beef, beef tartare is usually topped with raw egg and surrounded by French fries. Rye bread is usually served with this dish as well. In general, the term "tartare" can be used for other kinds of raw meat, such as horsemeat or fish. This dish was first created and served in France. Now, it's popular all-over Europe and America. Despite its name "tartare", this dish has nothing to do with tartare people who live in Asia. Beef tartare is usually categorized as an appetizer, which tends to be a small portion and more **delicate**.

● 韃靼牛肉

韃靼牛肉是由稍加調味過的洋蔥及生牛肉所組成，常在其上加上生蛋，並與薯條一同裝盤上桌。黑麥麵包也常與這道菜做搭配。一般來說，「韃靼」一詞可用於其他生肉料理，例如馬肉或魚。這道菜起源於法國，起初只於法國的餐廳供應，但現在於歐洲和美國都相當普遍。雖然其名為「韃靼」，但此道菜與亞洲韃靼民族並無關聯。韃靼牛肉一般被分類為開胃菜，因此份量通常較小且精緻。

字彙補充包

raw **adj** 生的；未煮的	enticing **adj** 引人食慾的
garnish **v** 裝飾	stem **n** 植物的莖
peep at　偷瞄	ever since　自從
miserably **adv** 悲慘地	make up one's mind 下定決心
take time　花時間；慢慢來	elevate **v** 提升；提高
careless **adj** 粗枝大葉的	glimpse **n** 一瞥
drip **v** 滴落	blade **n** 刀鋒
splash **v** 噴；濺；灑	stunned **adj** 嚇呆的
burst out laughing 捧腹大笑	sincerity **n** 真誠；真心
be composed of　由…組成	delicate **adj** 細緻的；精緻的

Part**1** 美食異國情緣篇

Part**2** 美食口語強化篇

Hot chocolate
熱巧克力

Every time I have a **fight** with Jean, I come here. "Lily of the Lake" is the name of the coffee shop, but I don't drink coffee. I choose hot chocolate every time.

Jean is stupid, and as far as I know, I'm stupid to be with him for the last three years. Deep in my heart, I know that he is **brilliant**, and that I'm so **attracted to** him. **Somehow**, part of me just can't be **convinced** that he is the perfect man for me. That's why I always **retreat** to "Lily of the Lake" for **refuge**. I find **shelter** here.

Whenever my lips touch the sticky liquid, a special chemical **simultaneously** grabs me and throws me into another **zone**. The salty mix with the bitter-sweet chocolate taste is like tear drops **rolling** down my throat.

As I think back on our relationship, Jean always appears on the corner of the street, looking for me. And that brings a smile to my face – see, there he is again.

Part1 美食異國情緣篇

　　每次我跟約翰有不愉快，我就會到這裡來。「湖邊的百合」是這家咖啡廳的名字。我不喝咖啡，我喝熱巧克力。

　　約翰很笨拙，但就我所知，我也是笨到極點了，才會跟他交往三年至今。在我心深處，我知道他是個很棒的人，而且我深受他吸引。但不知怎地，有一部分的我就是沒辦法承認他是我要的那一位。這就是為什麼我總是逃到「湖邊的百合」歇腳，在這裡，我找到庇蔭處。

Part2 美食口語強化篇

　　每當我的嘴唇碰到那黏稠的液體時，一種特別的感覺立即攫住我，並將我拋入另一個時空；那混合著苦澀與香甜的鹹味，就如眼淚般簌簌滑下我的喉嚨。而每次當我思考著我們的關係時，約翰總會出現在街角，四下張望著找我。看著他的身影，我總不禁莞爾，而——瞧，他又出現了。

● Hot chocolate

Hot chocolate varies from region to region, country to country. French hot chocolate is usually considered very thick and creamy. **Instead of** using chocolate powder, they **melt chunks** of chocolate; instead of water, they use milk. As a **result** of the mixture of bitter-sweet chocolate and milk, the drink is super **intense**. It can absolutely **fill one up** from noon to evening. In Italy, hot chocolate **tends to** be more simple: more chocolate added, therefore thicker, and a pinch of expresso powder. In Mexico one may find the most exciting hot chocolate: **crushed** spices beaten in hot chocolate. The end result is a foamy, spicy and creamy perfection.

● 熱巧克力

熱巧克力會因地區及國家而有許多不同的表現。法式熱巧克力普遍被認為是又濃又稠；法國人用塊狀巧克力取代沖泡巧克力粉，並用鮮奶取代白開水。苦甜巧克力及鮮奶的調和結果，便是濃郁且滋味深厚的巧克力飲品，飽足感可以一路從中午持續到傍晚。在義大利，熱巧克力比較單純，他們加入更多巧克力塊，因此更加濃稠，並會加入少許濃縮咖啡粉。墨西哥可能擁有最刺激的熱巧克力，也就是將現磨的香料混入手打熱巧克力中，滋味綿密、辛辣又濃郁。

 **字彙補充包**

fight	n 爭執、口角	brilliant	adj 出色的
be attracted to	受…吸引	somehow	不知怎地
convince	v 說服	retreat	v 撤退
refuge	n 避難所	shelter	n 收容所
simultaneously	adv 自發地	zone	n 領域、地區
roll	v 滑、滾	relationship	n 一段感情、關係
instead of	而不是…	melt	v 融化
chunk	n 塊	result	n 結果
intense	adj 激烈的	fill one up	使某人吃飽
tend to	v 傾向於	crush	v 壓、碾碎

Duck à l'orange
柳橙鴨

 情緣園地 MP3 *26*

Soft music, burning candles and the **chatters** of glasses – I have finally taken a girl to a restaurant like this! It doesn't matter how much it costs... well, actually, it does. I've been saving and **living poor** just for this meal. The waiter is kind enough to hand a menu without **price tags** to my partner; that's **wise**, because the price here almost gives me an **ulcer**. Excellent, they have **authentic** French **cuisine**. Cloe is a **foodie**; I will let her order to show my respect.

We have duck à l'orange and rose wine. How romantic! I'm actually dining with my angel in a French restaurant! Hmm, the duck is nicely done. I can still see the pink meat in the middle, that's awesome. The wine, wow, good choice! Cloe is **critiquing** the meat being overcooked. What is she talking about? Am I easily satisfied? Now she is commenting on how bad the rose wine it is. I can't believe this. She is ruining the dinner. She is leaving. Did she lose her mind? What a joke. Next time I should just come here alone.

　　輕音樂、搖曳的燭火還有玻璃杯的碰撞聲——我終於成功的帶著女孩子上這種餐館了！價錢不是重點……噢，沒有啦，其實為了吃這頓，我已經省吃儉用存錢了好一陣子。服務生真好，他給我的女伴的菜單是沒有標價錢的。真精明，因為這價錢幾乎要讓我得胃潰瘍了。好極了，他們有正統法國菜。克蘿伊很會品嘗美食，還是讓她點餐以示尊重吧。

　　我們點了柳橙鴨和粉紅酒。真浪漫呀！我真的跟我的天使在法式餐廳用餐耶！嗯嗯，這鴨料理得真不錯。中間的肉還是粉紅色的呢，非常好。至於這酒，哇，真搭！克蘿伊抱怨鴨肉煮得太老了，她是認真的嗎？該不會只有我傻傻地自足自滿吧？現在她換抱怨粉紅酒了，說味道不好。我真不敢相信！她毀了今天的晚餐！她要離開了，她瘋了嗎？搞什麼呀！下一次我還是自己來好了。

Duck à l'orange

It is said that this iconic French delicacy actually came from Italy, alone with the Medici family. No matter where its origin was, Duck à l'orange is absolutely a signature dish now in France and all-over the world. The recipe calls for Cointreau and Cognac, which add to the citrus flavor and elevate the taste. Parts of duck are stewed with herbs, onions, carrots and white wine for a long time, in order to produce the sauce that is poured over the duck. Usually, more than one kind of orange is used. This dish can be served with steamed potatoes, as well as rice.

● 柳橙鴨

據說這道極具代表性的法國佳餚，其實是梅第奇家族從義大利帶過來的。不論其出身地為何，柳橙鴨絕對是法國菜中的翹楚，且已遍傳全球。這道菜使用的君度橙酒和干邑白蘭地，提升了柳橙風味並讓味道更有層次。鴨的幾個部分會與香草、洋蔥、胡蘿蔔和白酒先燉煮過，用以製造淋在鴨肉上的醬汁。通常這道菜也會使用不只一種的柳橙。柳橙鴨一般搭配蒸煮的馬鈴薯或白飯。

 **字彙補充包**

chatter　**n** 聲響；震動	live poor　過貧窮的日子
price tag　**n** 價錢標籤	wise　**adj** 有智慧的
ulcer　**n** 潰瘍	authentic　**adj** 道地的；正統的
cuisine　**n** 美食；烹調	foodie　**n** 老饕
critique　**v** 批判；評論	overcook　**v** 煮得太過；煮過頭
satisfied　**adj** 滿足的	comment　**v** 評論；回應
ruin　**v** 毀壞；搞砸	lose one's mind　（人）發瘋
what a joke 搞什麼；搞笑嗎？	delicacy　**n** 佳餚
alone with　與…一起	signature　**n** 簽名；簽署
citrus　**adj** 柑橘類的	elevate　**v** 提升；升高

unit 27
Croque Madame
焗烤火腿乳酪吐司

 情緣園地 MP3 *27*

Feeling pretty proud of my French progress, I order Un croque-madame, s'il vous plait in French, of course, a dish I desperately need after an exhausted morning class.

Unluckily, something **strikes** me the next second and **destroys** my pride completely: I forgot to bring the money! I can't believe this is happening to me. I stand at the counter, **feeling like** crying. "There, it's my treat." Enzo's voice comes from behind. I turn around. "You **came from nowhere!**" I **gasp**, **holding back** the tears. "Well, I guess I'm the **lifesaver** now." He grins, and we walk toward the same table holding our trays. Now, savoring the creamy, egg-**soaked** toast, I feel that something more than friendship is **fermenting** - maybe something called love.

　　對自己法語進步速度感到相當有自信，我點了焗烤火腿乳酪吐司，一道在令人感到筋疲力盡的早上課程後迫切需要的菜餚。

　　不幸的是，下一秒便發生了徹底摧毀我自信心的慘事：我忘記帶錢了！真不敢相信這種事發生在我身上！我站在結帳台前，感覺快哭了。「喂，我請客。」安佐的聲音從身後傳來。我轉過身去，「你從哪冒出來的啊！」我倒抽一口氣說，強忍著淚水。「呵，我想我救了你一命哩。」現在，品嘗著香濃、流淌著蛋汁的焗烤火腿乳酪吐司，我感到友情以外的某個元素正在發酵。也許，是愛情吧。

● Croque Madame

"Croque" means "crack!" in French. It describes the sound when one bites into this crispy-juicy grilled toast. Croque Madame is made of two slices of bread, ham, Emmental cheese, white cream sauce and a sunny egg. First, **sandwich** the ham, cheese and sauce between two slices of bread, then fry or grill it until the cheese is melted. Sometimes, **additional** cheese is spread on top for a creamier taste. A sunny egg is added just before serving. The running egg yolk gives Croque Madame a unique rich, eggy, and creamy taste. Another similar **version** is Croque Monsieur, which is made exactly the same way without the sunny egg.

● 焗烤火腿乳酪吐司

Croque 法文意指「喀滋！」，形容咬下這道多汁又酥脆的烤土司時所發出的聲音。焗烤火腿乳酪吐司是以兩片吐司、火腿、伊蒙達乳酪、奶油白醬及一顆太陽蛋所組成。首先，將火腿、乳酪和白醬夾在兩片麵包中間，接著煎或烤至乳酪融化。有時候會在表面再撒上更多起司，讓吐司更濃郁。太陽蛋在上桌前才放上。流淌的蛋液使焗烤火腿乳酪吐司增添豐富、濃郁、奶香的獨特口感。另一道相似的料理叫 croquet Monsieur，是以一模一樣的原料及方法製成，惟獨沒有加上太陽蛋。

字彙補充包

order ⓥ 點餐	be proud of 以…自豪
progress ⓝ 進步	strike ⓥ 擊中；使…有印象
destroy ⓥ 摧毀	feel like 想要；好像快…
come from nowhere 突然冒出來	gasp ⓥ 喘息
hold back 忍住	lifesaver ⓝ 救命恩人
make fun of 取笑；嘲弄	soak ⓥ 浸泡
ferment ⓥ 發酵	sandwich ⓥ 將…夾在中間
additional ⓐⓓⓙ 額外的	version ⓝ 版本

Part 1 美食異國情緣篇

Part 2 美食口語強化篇

unit 28

Fish and Chips
炸魚薯條

As a **foreign** student, London is not very friendly to me. It rains all the time. What causes me **melancholy** is not only weather, but also food. I miss hot food, fresh vegetables and savory soups. One day, Loran caught me after class and **asked me out**.

Loran is **born and raised** in London, but he doesn't **possess** the **arrogance** that some British people have. I said yes **delightedly**. We went to the art museum, café and the park. **At the end of the day**, he told me to try some fish and chips. If it was not for the day, I'd have **rejected**. Nevertheless, the fresh fried fish and chips were not only crispy, but also refreshing. I never knew that junk food could be so good! "The secret is salt and malt vinegar." Loran explained with pride. People might call it food therapy, but for me, Loran was the cure for my sickness.

　　對我這個留學生而言，倫敦並不友善；這裡老是在下雨。讓我憂鬱的還不只是天氣，還有食物。我想念熱騰騰的飯、新鮮蔬菜和滋味馥郁的湯品。一天，羅倫在下課後約我出去。

　　羅倫是土生土長的倫敦人，但他沒有一些英國人抱持的傲慢。我開心的答應了他。我們去了美術館、咖啡廳和公園。最後，羅倫帶我嘗試炸魚薯條。若不是當天太愉快，我一定會拒絕的。然而，剛炸好的炸魚薯條不僅酥脆，更是令我耳目一新。我從不知道垃圾食物是這麼美味！「祕訣就在鹽巴和麥醋。」羅倫驕傲地解釋說。有人會稱此為食療，但對我而言，羅倫才是我的那帖良藥。

美食重點介紹

◉ Fish and Chips

Originated in Great Britain, fish and chips can now also be found in the USA, Australia and many European countries. Sauce and **cookery vary**. In Great Britain, **cod** is the most common fish in use, thanks to the geographic **circumstances** of being an island. Fish are often **skinned**, breaded and fried in 180 degrees' oil. It is said that because of the death of Jesus Christ, **catholic** church **forbade** meat-eating on Friday. Hence, people turn to fish instead. Even today there is no such rule, the tradition of eating fish and chips on Friday nights is **passed on**.

◉ 炸魚薯條

炸魚薯條源自英國,但現在美國、澳大利亞和很多歐洲國家也吃得到。其沾醬及料理方式因地而異。在英國,因為地緣的關係,多使用鱈魚來料理。通常魚會去皮、包裹麵粉並放入 180 度的油中油炸。關於其由來,有一說是因為耶穌基督死後,天主教禁止信徒在週五吃肉。因此,人們轉而吃魚。儘管今天教條不復存在,週五晚上吃炸魚薯條的傳統卻流傳了下來。

字彙補充包

foreign n 外國人	melancholy n 憂鬱；哀傷
porridge n 麥片粥	ask sb. out 邀約某人
born and raised 土生土長的	possess v 擁有；持有
arrogance n 傲慢、自負	delightedly adv 開心地
at the end of the day 最終；最後	reject v 拒絕
therapy n 療法	cure n 治療；治癒
cookery n 烹調法	vary v 多變
cod n 鱈魚	circumstance n 情勢；環境
skinned adj 去皮的	catholic n 天主教；adj 天主教的
forbid v 禁止	pass on 傳承

Cottage Pie
農舍派

 *29*

It is another **gloomy** day. **In a blink of time**, my front yard is **paved** with snow. I have to **park** my truck in the garage. The snow causes trouble: vision is **blurred**, tires slide, all kinds of **dreadful** accidents take place. Soon enough I will have to **shovel** the snow on the roof and on my **driveway**.

Still, on this kind of day, good things happen. For example, making cottage pie! Before pulling out frozen ground beef and chopping onions, I called Alice. She will be here **by the time** the pie is done. So I cook up the beef, **simmer** it in tomato sauce, and top the pot with mashed potato. The fragrance of meat **circulates** in the air as the pie sits **tranquilly** in the oven. Alice arrives just in time. As I have expected, she is **overwhelmed** by the fabulous smell in the house. I know we will surely enjoy ourselves in the warm and cozy environment.

今天又是一個令人提不起勁的日子。很快地，前院就積滿了雪，我必須把卡車停到車庫裡去。雪總是帶來麻煩，比如視線不清啦、輪胎打滑啦，什麼意外都會發生。要不了多久我就必須到屋頂上去剷雪，還要把車道上的雪清乾淨。

話雖如此，這種日子還是會有好事的，例如說烤個農舍派。在我把牛肉從冷凍庫拿出來、並開始切洋蔥之前，我先打電話給愛麗絲。她會在派烤好之前抵達。於是我開始烹煮牛肉，將牛肉在番茄糊中燉煮，並在鍋頂鋪上馬鈴薯泥。當派安安靜靜地在烤箱中烘烤時，屋裡漸漸充滿了肉煮熟的香氣。愛麗絲準時到了。就如我預期的一樣，她對屋裡美妙的香味感到又驚又喜。我知道我們一定會在溫暖又舒適的屋裡度過美好的一晚。

美食重點介紹

● Cottage Pie

Also known as Shepherd's Pie, cottage pie is a meat pie with potato topping instead of a crust. Usually, beef or lamb is used in a cottage pie, along with tomato paste, peas and carrots. It is said that "cottage" refers to cattle, thus beef is involved. Shepherd, on the other hand, refers to sheep. That's why lamb is the other ingredient in this recipe. Cottage pie is also a good way to deal with leftovers: just combine cooked meat and veggies, then top with mash potato! After a long time in the oven, flavors come together and a masterpiece is thus produced.

● 農舍派

農舍派又名牧羊人派，這是一種用馬鈴薯泥取代派皮的肉派。通常使用牛肉或羊肉，並加入番茄糊、青豆和胡蘿蔔。據說，因為「農舍」一詞與牲口有關，因此使用牛肉；又因「牧羊人」一詞與羊有關，因此也使用羊肉。農舍派也是解決剩菜的好方法：將煮熟的肉和蔬菜放在一起，鋪上馬鈴薯泥就行了！經過長時間的烘烤，所有味道和諧的融在一起，美味的料理也就大功告成了。

字彙補充包

Part **1**

美食異國情緣篇

Part **2**

美食口語強化篇

gloomy **adj** 陰沉的；憂鬱的	pave　**v** 鋪；堆積
in a blink of time 形容時間極短	blur　**v** 使模糊
park　**v** 停車	shovel　**v** 鏟
dreadful　**adj** 可怕的；嚇人的	by the time　在…之前
driveway　**n** 車道	circulate　**v** 流通；流轉
simmer　**v** 煨；燉	overwhelm　**v** 壓倒；震懾
tranquilly　**adv** 平靜地	on the other hand　另一方面
involve　**v** 包含；牽扯	masterpiece　**n** 傑作；大作
deal with　對付；解決	

Karelian pasty
米派

 情緣園地 MP3 ▶ *30*

Since the first day I arrived in Helsinki, I've been **enduring** the food they have here. Sour bread, **tasteless** crackers – not a **single** thing I have here can possibly be called tasty. My fourth couchsurfing host, Sarah, was a bright and **energetic** woman. When I saw her driving toward me on the central **square**, I felt a warm feeling **welling** up within. Sarah **treated** me with fried sausages, freshly **tossed** green salad, and vanilla ice cream. I immediately fell in love with her. Not because of the food she **offered** me, but because of her **glittering** eyes and the gentle smile.

The next day, before I **departed for** the ferry, she treated me again with a wonderful breakfast: Karelian pastry. The pastry was warm, and I hadn't liked it since the first time I tasted it. However, warm Karelian pastry tasted fluffy, and the rice inside is creamy. "Take some on the road. It may save you at some point." She joked. That was when I told her I would come back and would like to have the rest of my life with her.

　　自從我第一天到達赫爾辛基，我就一直在忍受芬蘭的食物。酸味麵包、食之無味的餅乾，沒一樣食物會讓我覺得好吃。我的第四個沙發主人莎拉是位陽光有活力的女性。當我在中央廣場上，看著她的車向我開來時，我覺得有股暖意從心底深處湧出。莎拉招待我吃炒香腸、新鮮沙拉和香草冰淇淋。我立刻就愛上了她，不是因為她招待我的食物，而足因為她靈動的雙眼和溫暖的笑容。

　　次日，在我出發去搭渡輪前，她又再次招待我豐盛的早餐：芬蘭米派。米派是溫熱的。從我第一次吃到這種派起，我就不曾對它有好感。然而溫熱的米派卻嘗起來蓬鬆可口，內餡的米飯也很綿密。「帶些到路上吃吧，說不定會救你一命呢！」她開玩笑著說。就在那時候，我告訴撒拉我一定會回來，並請她嫁給我，與我共度一生。

● Karelian pastry

In Finland, rye is used in every pastry: bread, crackers, etc. To make Karelian pastry, first mix all-purpose flour and rye flour. The result is a brown-colored pastry skin. Cook the rice with whole-fat milk and fold in the rye pastry. Karelian pastry can be served warm or cold, depending on taste. Usually, when it's served hot, it goes with butter to add up more flavor. The filling, other than creamed rice, may also be shredded apples or mashed potatoes. Karelian pastry is one of the most common Finnish cuisine that can be seen and purchased in homes and in stores.

● 米派

在芬蘭，裸麥（黑麥）廣泛的被運用在麵粉製品中，比如麵包、餅乾等。要製作米派，需先混合普通麵粉與裸麥粉，其結果是一層棕色的派皮。接著，將米放在全脂鮮奶中煮熟，並包入裸麥派皮中。米派可冷食也可熱食，端看個人喜好；通常熱的米派會跟奶油一起食用以增添風味。至於內餡，除了奶粥之外，蘋果泥、馬鈴薯泥也可包入做餡。米派是芬蘭最常見的美食之一，不論是在家中或是在商店裡都隨處可見。

字彙補充包

endure	v 忍耐；忍受	tasteless	adj 無味的
single	adj 單一的	energetic	adj 有活力的
square	n 廣場	well	v 湧出
treat	v 招待	toss	v 拋；擲；甩
offer	v 提供	depart for	出發前往…
glittering	adj 閃亮的	fluffy	adj 蓬鬆的
at some point	某個時刻	etc	等等（前加逗號）
fold	v 摺疊；合攏	depend on	根據…
add up	增添	other than	除了…還有…
cuisine	n 烹飪；美食	purchase	v 購買

Salmon Chowder with Dill
鮭魚蒔蘿濃湯

 情緣園地 MP3 *31*

Tonight my host is a guy named Jouni. We only **exchanged** a few words online, and now I'm going to **spend the night** with a stranger, **plus** he is a man. I didn't even know what he looks like! Will he be a monster? Oh, traveling is all about the **courage**, isn't it?

Anyway, right now I'm at the **doorpost**. There's no **turning back**. The door opens, and a cute face **shows up** from the darkness. "Come on in! You must be **worn out!**" To my **relief**, Jouni has a nice **personality**. Being in his tiny apartment feels relaxed. He prepared salmon chowder for me. "What's special in here?" I ask curiously. "It's dill. We love dill here in Sweden." The soup is creamy and warm. Flakes of dill are like cute little grass in a white ocean. The more I sip on the soup, the less nervous I am.

Maybe not only the soup does magic, Jouni does it, too.

今晚我的宿主是一位名叫尤尼的男性；我們僅僅在網路上交換過隻字片語，然後我就要跟這個陌生人共度一宿還是個男人。我甚至不知他長得是圓是扁哩！說不定他是怪獸呢？噢，旅行就是要有膽量，不是嗎？

總之，我現在已經在人家家門口了，為時已晚。門開了，一張可愛的臉從黑暗中探出來。「快進來吧！你一定累壞了！」尤尼是個好人真讓我鬆了口氣，迷你的公寓也讓我很放鬆。他為我準備了鮭魚蒔蘿濃湯。「這道湯的特色是什麼？」我好奇地問。「蒔蘿。我們瑞典人叫喜歡蒔蘿了。」這道湯又濃郁又溫暖，一片片蒔蘿在奶油海裡像可愛的綠草。隨著濃湯一口口下肚，我的緊張也漸漸褪去；也許不只是湯的效力，而是尤尼施了魔法吧。

● Salmon Chowder with Dill

Salmon and dill is a classic combination in North Europe; they can both be spotted on sandwiches, in salad or served as main course. Usually, the soup calls for salmon filet. Chunks of potato, carrot and butter are the soul of the chowder. Dill is chopped and added as garnish as well as a refreshing touch. Because this soup can sometimes be very thick, mashed potato may also be served on the side, in order to go even better with it. Mashed potato coated with chowder will be soaked thoroughly, producing a creamy, hearty taste.

● 鮭魚蒔蘿濃湯

鮭魚和蒔蘿是北歐的一項經典組合，在三明治、沙拉裡都找得到，甚至可當主菜上桌。通常鮭魚蒔蘿濃湯使用整塊鮭魚排，切塊的馬鈴薯、胡蘿蔔及奶油則是湯的靈魂。蒔蘿切碎後成為湯的裝飾，同時也為濃湯增添一絲清爽。這道湯有時候煮得非常濃，這時候可以另外準備馬鈴薯泥，跟濃湯更搭。澆上濃湯的薯泥會被完全浸潤，因而製造出滑順、綿密的口感。

 字彙補充包

safe and sound　平安無事地	backpacker　n 背包客
accomplish　v 達成；完成	exchange　v 交換
spend the night　過夜	plus　adv 再加上…
courage　n 勇氣；膽量	doorpost　n 門前；門口
turn back　回頭；放棄	show up　n 出現；現身
wear out　使某人筋疲力竭	relief　n 放鬆；慰藉
personality　n 個性；人格	combination　n 組合；結合
spot　v 發現	main course　主餐
call for　要求	filet　n 魚排
coat with　以…包覆	thoroughly　adv 徹底地

 情緣園地　 MP3 32

It's hard to **neglect** waffle houses on the streets of Brussels. They are everywhere. I **am** not **crazy about** sugary sweets, but **it won't harm** to have a taste of the country. "Do you have any **recommendations?**" I ask my **escort**, Giada. Since there are so many, I want to have **the real deal**. "I'd suggest that we skip those fancy decorations and go for pure **genuineness**." She replies. Then she leads me to a small shop that people are **lining up** in front of.

"This is what we're looking for: a local crowd." She laughs. I came to Belgium for business, and Giada **accompanies** me wherever I go. Only three days together, I've started to like her. She is independent, professional and **humorous**. What a **glowing** precious woman. Hot waffles are delivered to our hands. The sugar is caramelized perfectly on the surface. With just one bite, the soft-chewiness has blown my mind. "Surprising, isn't it?" Giada chuckles. I guess she notices my astonishment, but I wish she wouldn't uncover the affection hidden in my eyes.

　　走在布魯塞爾街上，要忽視一間一間的鬆餅屋相當難；它們無所不在。我並不特別喜歡甜點，但淺嘗幾口倒是無傷大雅。「你有沒有推薦的店家呢？」我問我的導遊吉雅妲。鬆餅屋這麼多，我可不想踩雷。「我建議我們跳過那些華麗的配料，吃原味就好。」她回答道。她領著我到一家小店，門口列了長長的人龍。

　　「這就是我們要的：當地人最懂。」她笑說。我來比利時出公差，而吉雅妲無論到那兒都陪著我。僅僅相處三天，我就已經喜歡上她了。吉雅妲獨立自主、專業且幽默。多亮麗的一位可人兒啊！熱呼呼的格子鬆餅送到我們手上了，砂糖在表面形成完美的焦糖層。我才吃一口，那軟綿又有嚼勁的口感立刻叫我大吃一驚。「好吃得嚇人，是吧？」吉雅妲莞爾一笑。我想她注意到我的驚愕了，但我希望她可別發現我眼神裡的情意才好。

美食重點介紹

● Waffle

Waffles are identified by their square-shaped surface. Different from pancakes, these little pastries are crispier and easier to hold in hand. Waffles are originated in Europe, which are known as Liege waffle and Belgium waffle. Their shapes are slightly different, but both are popular with whipped cream, fruit and chocolate decorations. Plain waffles, however, may be the best way to taste this treat; a layer of caramel simply brings out the aroma of a wonderful pastry. Waffles are also common in the States and in Asia. Especially in Hong Kong, waffles have developed their own shape, like a bunch of eggs.

● 格子鬆餅

格子鬆餅因其一格一格的外型而擁有高辨識度。不同於美式熱鬆糕，這些小型糕點較酥脆，也較易用手取食。格子鬆餅源於歐洲，以列日鬆餅和比利時鬆餅最出名。這兩種鬆餅外型有些許不同，然而二者都能以打發鮮奶油、水果及巧克力裝飾。然而，原味可能是品嚐這種甜點最好的選擇，因為一層簡單的焦糖最能帶出一個鬆餅的好滋味。格子鬆餅在美國及亞洲也相當常見，尤其在香港，格子鬆餅儼然已發展出其獨創的外型：雞蛋仔。

字彙補充包

neglect **v** 忽略；忽視	be crazy about 不喜歡某事／物
it won't harm 也不會怎麼樣	recommendation **n** 推薦
escort **n** 嚮導	the real deal 好東西；真貨
genuineness **n** 真實；真正	line up 排隊
accompany **v** 陪伴	humorous **adj** 有幽默感的
glowing **adj** 閃耀的	blow one's mind away 使某人大開眼界
astonishment **n** 震驚；驚愕	uncover **v** 揭露；揭發
be identified by 以…來辨認	crispy **adj** 酥脆的
slightly **adv** 稍微	decoration **n** 裝飾
plain **adj** 平淡的；原味的	a bunch of 一大堆

Stroopwafel
焦糖煎餅

This thin, sticky cookie-waffle like dessert is **addictive**. My favorite way of eating stroopwafel is, **undoubtedly**, place it on top of a steaming hot coffee. After a while, the heat **melts down** the caramel inside the pastry. That's when I take it up, **appreciate** its beauty for a few seconds, and eat it. Aaron told me that my way of being **gourmet** is a little bit **erotic**. "**Shut your face**." I just laughed about it.

"It's like you're eating the most delicious food in the world." Aaron claimed. "That makes you look delicious too." **When it comes to** good food, I never **behave** gentle. And know what? Men that see me acting this way will always **fall for** me. Right now, Aaron is just like the melting caramel, **gradually** falling down the pastry – he will definitely fall in love with me.

　　這片薄薄黏黏、像餅乾又像鬆餅的甜點令人上癮。我最愛的焦糖煎餅吃法，不用說，當然是放在熱氣蒸騰的咖啡上。不消片刻，熱氣便會融化中間的焦糖夾層，這便是我拿起煎餅的時機；我會先花幾秒欣賞誘人的煎餅，接著一口吃下。艾倫告訴我，我大啖美食的樣子有點兒情色。「閉嘴啦。」我僅一笑置之。

　　「你好像在吃全世界最好吃的食物，」艾倫如是說。「這讓你看起來也變得秀色可餐。」談到美食，我可沒有女人的矜持，而猜怎麼著，往往看到我品嚐食物的男人也會拜倒在我的石榴裙下。現在的艾倫就像那要融不融的焦糖，逐漸滑下煎餅……他一定會愛上我的。

Part**1**
美食異國情緣篇

Part**2**
美食口語強化篇

● Stroopwafel

This is a world-famous Dutch dessert. It is made with two layers of thin wafers with caramel filling. The caramel is **stiff** at room temperature. However, once the Stroopwafel is placed on top of a hot drink, it starts melting slowly. Just-made Stroopwafel keeps its **fluid**, **gooey** sandwich filling, that can just be enjoyed right away. It is said that Stroopwafel was created by a pastry chef who didn't want to waste extra ingredients. Thus, with some sugar, butter and flour, Stroopwafel was **invented**. Store-bought Stroopwafel is cheap, **whereas** hand-made Stroopwafel has better quality.

● 焦糖煎餅

這是一個聞名世界的荷蘭甜點，由兩片輕薄的煎餅中間夾著焦糖製成。焦糖在室溫下為固態，但只要將焦糖煎餅放在熱飲上，過一會兒，焦糖便會慢慢融化。現做的焦糖煎餅仍保有液態、黏滑的內餡，可以當場享用。據說焦糖煎餅是由一位不願浪費多餘食材的糕餅師傅所發明，他用一點砂糖、奶油及麵粉製造了焦糖煎餅。商店販售的焦糖煎餅較便宜，但往往手工焦糖煎餅品質較佳。

字彙補充包

addictive **adj** 令人上癮的	undoubtedly **adv** 無庸置疑地
melt down　融化	appreciate **v** 欣賞；感激
gourmet **adj** 愛好美食的	erotic **adj** 情色的
shut one's face 閉上嘴（=shut up）	behave **v** 行為；表現
when it comes to　說到…	fall for　愛上；掉入陷阱
gradually **adv** 逐漸	fluid **adj** 液態的；流動的
stiff **adj** 僵硬的；僵直的	invent **v** 發明
gooey **adj** 黏稠的	quality **n** 品質
whereas　而…	

Part **1**
美食異國情緣篇

Part **2**
美食口語強化篇

143

Borscht

羅宋湯

 情緣園地 MP3 *34*

Andrew is a good friend of mine, and he **introduces** many things in Russia **to** me. Today, he invites me to do some **research** in his house. Andrew prepared traditional borscht and sour cream dill roll-ups. For me, everything is new. **In order to** be polite, even though I'm so **tempted** by all the good food, I do not just **dive into** the **delicacies** on the table.

"Do you know Russian Borscht?" Andrew asks. "Not really. The Borscht I know is made of tomato." **Frankly**, I respond. "That's a big mistake." He laughs. "Here, try it with some more sour cream." **A pile of** sour cream is scooped in my bowl. I take a breath and take a spoon. "It is so **flavorful**!" I **exclaim**. Andrew smiles lovingly. I have been traveling a lot, and my **instincts** tell me that at this moment, Andrew has a **purpose** in my life. Oh my, all I want to have is a friend!

　　安德魯是我的一位好友，他為我打開了認識俄羅斯的大門，我對此心懷感謝。這天，他邀請我到他家去做些研究。安德魯準備了傳統羅宋湯和酸奶蒔蘿卷。對我而言，一切都是那麼新奇，然而為了保持禮貌，儘管美食當前，我仍把持住自己，沒有立刻忘情大吃。

　　「你知道俄國羅宋湯嗎？」安德魯問道。「不太知道，我所認知的羅宋湯是番茄做的。」我老實回答。「那可是大誤解呢！」安德魯大笑，「加點酸奶一起品嘗吧！」説完就把　大匙酸奶舀到我的碗裡。我深深的吸了一口氣，接著吃了一匙。「好有滋味呀！」我讚嘆道，而安德魯則寵溺的笑起來。我已經旅行了一段時間，而這時直覺告訴我，安德魯想向我告白。天啊，我只想要一個好朋友而已啊！

● Borscht

Borscht originates in Ukraine, and it has become famous in East Europe **as time goes on**. The basic ingredients for borscht are beets, salt, sugar and lemon juice. In Russia, Borscht is usually based on beef broth. Carrots, potatoes and spinach are common in the soup. The recipe has **developed** itself in many countries. In Shanghai, Borscht has been introduced by immigrants. The **residents** of Shanghai **replaced** beet with tomato, and more sugar is added to **balance** the **acidity**. It is said that if there are one hundred Shanghainese, there will be one hundred different ways of making Borscht.

● 羅宋湯

羅宋湯起源自烏克蘭,並隨時間推移漸漸流行到東歐地區。羅宋湯的基本原料為甜菜、鹽、糖和檸檬汁。在俄國,羅宋湯通常以牛肉湯為基底,胡蘿蔔、馬鈴薯及菠菜是常見的湯料。在不同的國家有不同的做法。在上海,羅宋湯是由移民引進。當地居民以番茄取代甜菜,並加入更多糖來平衡酸味;有一説為一百個上海人會有一百種羅宋湯做法。

字彙補充包

introduce A to B 將 A 介紹給 B	grateful **adj** 感激的
research **n** 研究	time for... 該是…的時間了
in order to 為了	tempt **v** 引誘
dive into 開動	delicacy **n** 美食
frankly **adv** 坦白說	a pile of 一疊；一堆
flavorful **adj** 美味的	exclaim **v** 讚嘆
instinct **n** 直覺	purpose **n** 目的
as time goes on 隨著時間過去	develop **v** 發展
resident **n** 居民	replace A with B 以 A 取代 B
balance **v** 使平衡	acidity **n** 酸性

Part **1** 美食異國情緣篇

Part **2** 美食口語強化篇

unit
35

Danish Pastry
丹麥麵包

"Hey, have you ever felt being **discriminated against**?" I asked Deanna. She is a Latino, which means she is a foreigner, too, **more or less**. "Well, you know, you can't **please** everybody." She responds, with a latte in her hand. "I know it's impossible, but these – Parisians really **piss me off**." I say in a low **tone** so other people won't notice.

"Like, how much can you **tolerate** if you're always **made fun of**?" I look right into her eyes, trying to find some **sympathy** there. She looks back at me and suddenly smiles. "Here, have a Danish pastry." She pushes a bag in front of me. That's **fishy**. "Danish pastry doesn't come from Denmark. They just **fake it**. Who cares? It tastes good. That's what **counts**." She suddenly leans forward and gives me a kiss. I guess she's got that spell on me.

「喂，你有沒有感覺受歧視過啊？」我問狄安娜，她是拉丁女孩，也就是說她在某種程度上也是個外國人。「嗯，你知道，你是無法取悅所有人的。」她說，一手捧著拿鐵咖啡。「我知道不可能，但這些──巴黎佬，真的讓我很生氣。」我壓低聲音說道，避免引起旁人的注意。

「這樣說好了，如果你總是被取笑，你能忍耐多久？」我望進她眼裡，想從那兒找到一絲同情。她回望我，並突然微笑起來。「喂，吃個丹麥麵包吧。」她將一個袋子推到我面前來，我頓時金剛二丈摸不著頭緒。「丹麥麵包不是從丹麥來的，只是以訛傳訛。但，誰在乎呢？麵包好吃，這就夠了。」她突然傾身向前吻了我，我想我中了她的魔咒了。

美食重點介紹

● Danish pastry

Despite its name, Danish pastry actually came from Austria and flourished in Denmark. In Europe, there are roughly two kinds of bread: thin bread and rich bread. Contrary to thin bread, which is made of flour, water and salt, rich bread contains a lot of butter and sugar. Danish pastry belongs to the latter. Among European countries, especially in France, Danish pastry is popular for breakfast. A typical French breakfast includes croissant, a cup of café au lait, and some fruit. In Italy, Danish pastry goes perfectly with dark, strong, powerful expresso.

● 丹麥麵包

其名饒富興味，丹麥麵包其實源自奧地利，而在丹麥發揚光大。在歐洲，麵包可粗略分為兩種：「瘦麵包」和「滋養麵包」。「瘦麵包」多以麵粉、水及鹽巴為組成成分，與此相反的「滋養麵包」則包含大量的奶油和砂糖；丹麥麵包正屬後者。在歐洲，特別是法國，丹麥麵包十分常見於早餐。一份典型的法式早餐包括可頌麵包、一杯牛奶咖啡和一些水果。在義大利，丹麥麵包和濃黑、渾厚又強勁的濃縮咖啡十分速配。

字彙補充包

racist　n 種族主義者	immigrant　n 移民
discriminate against　v 歧視	more or less　某種程度上
please　v 取悅	piss sb. off　使（人）生氣
tone　n 語調	tolerate　v 忍受
make fun of　取笑	sympathy　n 憐憫心
fishy　adj 可疑的	fake sth.　（假裝做）某事
sth. count　（某事）算數	lean　v 傾身
spell　n 咒語	flourish　v 發揚
roughly　adv 粗略	contrary to　與…相反
contain　v 包含	the latter　後者

Frankfurter Sausage
法蘭克福香腸

 情緣園地 MP3 36

Being pen pals for 6 months, I'm paying Ben a visit. He told me that hot dogs in the United States aren't equal to Frankfurter sausage. Ben promises to take me to a restaurant for real sausage.

As far as I know, German dudes are **stubborn** (**comparatively**), **eloquent** and extremely proud of their culture. I think it's strange, but I'**m drawn to** their men and their culture. Ben is tall and **skinny**. Sometimes I look at him **from a distance**, and find he **resembles** a sausage. I didn't tell him this, of course. The restaurant is an all-you-can-eat buffet. My eyes are wide open when I **spot** dozens of different sausages lying there, with sauerkraut and picked cabbage, all those mouth-watering **morsels**. I realize that the German diet is actually like their people:

tough, hard-to-beat, and tasty.

當了六個月的筆友後，我拜訪了班。他告訴我美國熱狗不等同法蘭克福香腸。他說會帶我去真正的香腸餐廳。

目前為止，我認為德國人相當頑固（比較起來啦！），好辯且對自己的文化極端自負。對此，相當神奇的是，我無法否認自己受其吸引。班又高又瘦，有時候遠遠的看他，我會覺得他就像根香腸似的；這我當然不會告訴他。他帶我去一家吃到飽餐廳，看到十幾二十種的香腸，我眼睛睜得老大。還有德國酸菜、醃漬高麗菜等等，各種各樣令人口水直流的美味。我發現德國的飲食其實就像德國人：實在、難以抗拒、而且美味。

● Frankfurter Sausage

Germany is known as a country of "sausage and beer". Truly, sausage alone is widely **consumed** in Germany, and it also **fascinates** Germany's European neighbors and the United States. Frankfurter sausage, as one of those famous ones, is made with pure pork. It is considered that it should be boiled only and is usually served with mustard, horseradish and mashed potato. Many families **boast** their own recipes for making sausage. Spices, percentage of meat and fat, cooking time, etc, can cause a huge difference between those familiar-looking sausages. Finding and savoring the differences in each restaurant is always a delicious **adventure** in Germany.

● 法蘭克福香腸

德國是一個以「香腸和啤酒」聞名的國家。的確,香腸不僅在德國境內銷量高,也風靡德國的臨近歐洲國家及美國。身為眾多出名的香腸之一,法蘭克福香腸是以純豬肉製成。通常認為這種香腸只適合水煮,並與芥末、山葵和馬鈴薯泥一同享用。許多家庭以自家秘製香腸為傲;香料、肥瘦肉比例及烹煮時間等,都能讓這些外貌相似的香腸產生不同的食感。搜尋並品嘗各家餐廳不同的香腸，是拜訪德國的一場美味冒險。

字彙補充包

contemptuous **adj** 輕蔑的	equal to　與…相等
confuse **v** 混淆	claim **v** 主張
pen pal **n** 筆友	virtual **adj** 虛擬的
stubborn **adj** 固執的	comparatively **adv** 比較上
eloquent **adj** 辯才無礙的	be drawn to　受…吸引
skinny **adj** 過瘦的	from a distance　從遠處
resemble **v** 與…相像	spot **v** 發現；看到
morsel **n** 塊（此指菜餚）	tough **adj** 堅忍的
consume **v** 消耗	fascinate **v** 吸引
boast **v** 以…自豪	adventure **n** 冒險

Flaki
牛肚湯

 情緣園地 MP3 ▸ 37

Every family in Poland cooks Flaki, but somehow, the overwhelming smell of it is just disgusting to me. Ola is my girlfriend. We started **seeing each other** a few weeks ago and she comes to my place **frequently**.

Despite the fact that I dislike Flaki, she cooks it all the time. One of the reasons that I like her is that she is always true to herself. Nevertheless, it would be more **thoughtful** of her if she just cooks in her own place. The strong **scent** of cattle **tripe** is **lingering** in the whole place: bedroom, bathroom, everywhere.

I am **irritated** and I walk toward her angrily. "You must be tired!" Ola suddenly turns to me with a smile, "Here, some hot soup will help you." Something **inexplicable** enlightens me and I sit down submissively. That day, Flaki finally became tasty.

　　每個波蘭家庭都會烹調牛肚湯，但不知為何，牛肚湯詭異的味道讓我覺得噁心。歐拉是我的女友，我們幾週前開始交往後，她便很常到我家來。

　　雖然我不喜歡，她卻老是在煮這道湯。我喜歡她的其中一個理由，就是她相當忠於自我。話雖如此，她若是只在她家煮，那可貼心多了。烹煮牛肚的強烈臭味在整個家縈繞不去，臥室、廁所，到處都是。

　　被惹惱的我怒氣沖沖地走向歐拉，「你一定累了吧！ 沒想到她微笑著轉向我說：喝點熱湯會對你有幫助的。」某種無法解釋的事物在那時照亮了我，因此我順服地坐下。那天，牛肚湯終於變得美味可口了。

● Flaki

This is a traditional Polish soup. The main ingredient in the soup is tripe, usually beef. First **simmer** the whole tripe in boiling water for about 20 minutes to remove the overwhelming smell. This will cause a strong and **aggressive odor** that lasts for hours, which is to some people **unbearable**. Then, the **roux** is made in a pan with oil and flour. Soon the roux is added in a new pot of clean tripe, water and **multiple** spices. The unique flavor of flaki comes from the stewed tripe and marjoram, an **original** spice of Poland. Flaki is best served with meatballs, rolls and bread.

● 牛肚湯

這是一道傳統波蘭湯品。這道湯的主要材料牲口的胃部,通常是牛肚。首先,將整片牛肚放進滾水中,沸騰約二十分鐘以去除腥味。這道程序會產生強烈且難聞的氣味,而且幾小時內不會消散;有的人認為此氣味十分難以忍受。然後,在平底鍋中燒熱油及麵粉,製作油糊。將油糊加入一乾淨湯鍋,放入清理過的牛肚、水和數種香料。牛肚湯獨特的香氣來自燉煮的牛肚和一種波蘭特有的香料:墨角蘭。牛肚湯和肉丸、小餐包或麵包片都相當速配。

字彙補充包

wrinkle　**v** 皺起	appreciate　**v** 喜歡；欣賞
see sb.　與某人交往	frequently　**adv** 頻繁地
despite the fact that...　儘管	thoughtful　**adj** 體貼的
scent　**n** 氣味	tripe　**n** 肚子
linger　**v** 縈繞；盤旋	irritated　**adj** 被激怒的
inexplicable　**adj** 無法解釋的	enlighten　**v** 啟發
submissively　**adv** 順服地	simmer　**v** 熬、煨
aggressive　**adj** 侵略性的	odor　**n** 氣味
unbearable　**adj** 無法忍受的	roux　**n** 油糊（料理術語）
multiple　**adj** 多種的	original　**adj** 原創的

Churro
吉拿棒

38

情緣園地　MP3　38

　　I've been looking for the one to spend the rest of my life with for a while. Now I'm **parking** outside of a **reputable chocolatier**, **fingers crossed**. Carrie and I got to know each other on a dating website. After **countless** photo **deceptions** and **ridiculous** dates, I can only pray that this one **nails it**. There's a woman walking towards me⋯oh no, is that Carrie? She said she'd wear a red dress. God, please, don't be⋯she's huge! I think I should wave⋯she just **turns away**?

　　Oh boy, the **gorgeous** woman waving at me inside must be Carrie. Thank God! She looks **in shape** and healthy. I **hop in** the store in a hurry. I notice that Carrie already ordered a plate of churros and two cups of chocolate. "You like churros?" I asked, **trembling** with excitement. Carrie is confident, beautiful and loquacious, I can't believe it. What is happening now is for real. "I do! Do you? I think it goes well with bittersweet chocolate." She chatters, with her beautiful finger dipping a churro in her cup. This is it, I say to myself. I've hit the jackpot.

Part 1
美食異國情緣篇

Part 2
美食口語強化篇

　　我在尋找能跟我共度一生的人，已經找了一段時間。現在，我正停車在一間有名的巧克力店外面，手指交叉祈禱著。卡莉和我是在約會網站上認識的，而在無數的假照片和荒謬的約會之後，我只能祈禱這次讓我找到對的人。有個女人朝我走過來了…噢不，那是卡莉嗎？她說她會穿紅色的洋裝。神啊，拜託告訴我那不是，她也太胖了吧！我想我該揮揮手…咦，她轉彎了？

　　喔天啊，那位坐在店裡向我揮手的美麗女人一定是卡莉。感謝上天！她看起來身材勻稱且健康。我急急忙忙走進店內，發現卡莉已經點了一盤吉拿棒和兩杯熱巧克力。「你喜歡吉拿棒嗎？」我因為興奮而顫抖著問道。卡莉是個自信、美麗又健談的女人，我簡直不敢相信現在正在發生的一切是真實的。「喜歡啊！你呢？我覺得吉拿棒跟苦甜巧克力很搭。」她格格笑著說，一邊用她修長美麗的手指將吉拿棒浸入杯中的巧克力裡。我心想，就是她，我中頭獎了！

◉ Churro

Churro is a Spanish fried pastry. The dough itself **resembles** the one for donuts, but after it's fried, the center becomes **hollow**. There are many ways of serving churros: serving plain is the most popular way. Since there is always a cup of bittersweet chocolate (60% or up, sugar on the side), unsweetened churros fit it better. However, there are also churros that are coated with confectioner's sugar, stuffed with chocolate, custard or caramel. The variation **goes on**. Some believe that churro was introduced from China in 16th century, but the fact is still under **discussion**.

◉ 吉拿棒

吉拿棒是一種西班牙的油炸點心。生麵團跟甜甜圈的麵團十分相似，然而油炸後，吉拿棒中間會呈空心狀。吉拿棒有許多變化，而原味吉拿棒是最受歡迎的。通常享用吉拿棒時都會搭配苦甜巧克力飲品（60%或以上的巧克力，砂糖另附），未沾砂糖的吉拿棒與之最速配。然而，有的吉拿棒沾滿糖粉，有的填入巧克力、卡士達餡或焦糖，變化相當多。有些人相信吉拿棒是在十六世紀從中國傳入的，但真相如何還有待商榷。

字彙補充包

park **v** 停車	reputable **adj** 有信譽的
chocolatier **n** 巧克力專門店	fingers crossed　祈禱、求好運
countless **adj** 無數的	deception **n** 騙局；欺騙
ridiculous **adj** 荒唐的	nail it　成功做到某事
turn away　轉身、撇開	gorgeous **adj** 美麗的；燦爛的
in shape　身材良好	hop in　急急忙忙進入…
tremble **v** 顫抖	loquacious **adj** 健談的
hit the jackpot 中樂透、頭獎	resemble **v** 與…類似
hollow **adj** 中空的	fit **v** 與…搭配
go on　繼續進行	discussion **n** 討論

Part **1**
美食異國情緣篇

Part **2**
美食口語強化篇

Tomato Garlic Bread
番茄大蒜麵包

 情緣園地 MP3 39

Ever since I met him, he had been so confident. Everything to him is like **a piece of cake**. I look closely to David's hands, trying to **record** the secret recipe of making this **knockout** tomato garlic bread. I was born and raised in England. The **lousy** weather pushed me out of the country.

Spain; however, seems to be the **opposite**. Everything is so bright and warm. People here boast about their cuisine, which I have to admit that they've got a reason to. To me, David keeps **dragging** me toward him like a **magnet**. I'm **timid** and he is bright; he is the sun and I'm the moon. I'm not sure if he has feelings about me, but just being with him gives me **warmth** and **strength**. "it's coming out of the oven!" David **cheers**. The olive oil and tomato juice are glowing on the hot toast, and David is just the shining star of mine.

　　自從我們相識，他就總是這麼自信滿滿，每件事對他來說似乎都易如反掌。我仔細地盯著大衛的手，試著記下這道「驚世番茄大蒜麵包」的秘密配方。我是土生土長的英國人，糟糕的天氣讓我出走。

　　然而，西班牙就像另一個相反的國度：這裡的一切都是閃耀又溫暖的。人們以西班牙菜自豪，我也承認他們的確有理由這麼做。對我來說，大衛就像不斷吸引我靠近的磁石。我很內向，他卻外放；他像太陽，我是月亮。我不確定他對我是否有情，但僅僅待在他身邊，我就獲得溫暖和力量。「出爐囉！」大衛歡呼。橄欖油和番茄的汁液在熱呼呼的麵包上閃耀，而大衛則是我的亮麗巨星。

Part **1**
美食異國情緣篇

Part **2**
美食口語強化篇

Tomato Garlic Bread

In Spain, tomato and garlic are widely used in almost every dish. To make this bread, first drizzle olive oil over sliced bread. Grill the bread or toast it until golden brown. Then, rub raw garlic on the crispy bread. The heat will melt down the garlic gradually, leaving the aromatic garlic flavor. The last step is to rub fresh tomato over the bread. Then season it with salt and pepper to taste. This is a delightful snack and afternoon refreshment. As an appetizer, the freshness wakens the taste buds, making room for dishes to come. The usage of olive oil in place of butter gives it a lighter taste, too.

◉ 番茄大蒜麵包

在西班牙，幾乎所有料理中，番茄和大蒜都被廣泛地運用。要製作這道烤麵包，首先將橄欖油撒在切片的麵包上，接著將麵包烤到金黃酥脆。之後，取生大蒜抹在麵包上。麵包的熱氣會逐漸將蒜末融化，進而產生芬芳的大蒜香氣。最後的步驟是取新鮮番茄「刷」在麵包上，然後以鹽和胡椒調味。這是道美味的零嘴或下午點心，作為開胃菜，其清爽的滋味喚醒味蕾，便於品嘗接下來的主餐。使用橄欖油取代奶油，也使這道麵包的口味更顯輕盈。

字彙補充包

a piece of cake　易如反掌之事	record　**v** 紀錄
knockout　**adj** 傑出的	lousy　**adj** 糟糕的
opposite　**adj** 相反的	drag　**v** 拉；拽
magnet　**n** 磁鐵	timid　**adj** 害羞的
warmth　**n** 溫暖	strength　**n** 力量
cheer　**v** 歡呼	widely　**adv** 廣泛地
rub　**v** 抹、擦	refreshment　**n** 零食
waken　**v** 使覺醒	make room for　給…空間
usage　**n** 使用；利用	in place of　取代

unit 40

Sachertorte
薩赫蛋糕

 情緣園地 MP3 40

"Jack, this is for you." Like a **tornado**, Natasha shows up in my classroom, **lands** a package of cake on my desk and departs. She always **makes my head spin**. No matter how many times I tell her that I don't fancy sweets, she never stops giving out her **chef d'oevre**. Unlike me, many **peers** of mine are fans of Natasha's creations. I hate this **ritual** of accepting desserts I don't want from Natasha. I don't eat them and my classmates circle me like **scavenger** birds looking for a bite.

I open the package, and there is a sachertorte. It's dark, chocolatey, and sweet **visually**. As I start **giving it out** piece by piece, a thought suddenly comes to my mind: why don't I take a piece? I cut off an **edge** of sachertorte, expecting the **explosion** of a sugary bomb.

To my surprise, the first thing I taste is bitterness. It strikes me at the moment, that Natasha must feel the same bitterness due to my neglect and ungratefulness. I bounce up, and like an arrow, I'm out on the corridor rushing toward her.

「傑克，這個給你。」娜塔莎像旋風一樣的出現在我的教室，放了個蛋糕在桌子上後又倏地離開。她總是搞得我暈頭轉向。不管我告訴她幾次我不愛甜食，她從未停止送我她的蛋糕作品。我的死黨們倒跟我不同，喜歡她蛋糕的大有人在。娜塔莎送我蛋糕的慣例讓我感到不舒服，我不吃蛋糕，而我的同學們總像禿鷹一樣環繞著我，等著分一杯羹。

打開盒子，裡面是一個薩赫蛋糕。看起來黑嘛嘛的、很「巧克力」、一副很甜的樣子。就在我一片片送出蛋糕之際，我突然靈光一閃：為什麼不自己吃一片呢？於是我切了蛋糕一角，預備接受砂糖炸彈的衝擊。令我驚訝的是，最先嘗到的味道卻是苦味。那時，我突然懂了；因著我的漠視、不珍惜，娜塔莎想必也嚐到同樣的苦味。我跳了起來，像支箭一般衝下走廊，往我的親愛女孩那兒直奔。

◉ Sachertorte

Invented accidentally by an apprentice in Vienna, sachertorte now has become one of the most recognized desserts in the world. "Torte" means cake in German, and Sacher is the family name of its inventor. Traditionally, sachertorte is composed of two layers of dense chocolate cake, which sandwich apricot jam in the middle. Chocolate ganache is a finishing touch for the cake. Since this cake is rich and intense by itself, usually it is served with unsweetened whipped cream. About the origin and the when the earliest Sachertorte appears, there are still debates.

◉ 薩赫蛋糕

薩赫蛋糕是在維也納被一位糕點學徒意外發明出來的，然而，如今已成了世上最有知名度的甜點之一。『torte』一詞德文原意蛋糕，而 Sacher 則是發明者的姓氏。薩赫蛋糕傳統的作法，是由兩片紮實的巧克力蛋糕間夾上杏桃果醬，外層淋上巧克力甘納許所製成。因為蛋糕本身甜度相當高，因此通常配不甜的打發鮮奶油。關於薩赫蛋糕的來源和最早出現的時間，目前仍有許多爭議。

 **字彙補充包**

tornado **n** 颶風	land **v** 降落
make one's head spin 令人暈頭轉向	chef d'oeuvre **n** 大師之作
peer **n** 同儕	ritual **n** 慣例
scavenger **n** 清道夫	visually **adv** 視覺上
give out 分送	edge **n** 邊緣
explosion **n** 爆炸	due to 因為
neglect **n** 忽視	bounce **v** 彈跳
corridor **n** 長廊	apprentice **n** 學徒
recognize **v** 認可；認出	be composed of 以…組成
dense **adj** 稠密的	debate **n** 爭論

unit
41

Pirozhki
油炸包

 情緣園地   MP3 41

"Sardines in a can" might just be me right now. Standing on the train, being **squeezed** from every direction, and the worst, people are smoking in here. **What on earth** makes the government **permit** people to smoke on the train? **Unbelievable!** Commuting is such a daily **despair**. After I finally get off the train, I see Rose waiting at the ticket **kiosk**. Rose is my coworker. We **happen to** live in the same area, thus get off at the same train station.

Working in the city and being forced to commute is horrible. I had the idea to move in the city before, but since I know Rose had to commute too, I **gave up** the idea just to see her every day. We **greet each other** and start walking to work. Being with Rose always makes me feel comfortable, I think she feels the same. "Hey, you have breakfast yet?" She suddenly asks, and hesitantly hands me a paper bag. It's Pirozhki! "I made them." She grins, timidly. What a surprise! Although I don't want to move on recklessly, this little move certainly touched my heart.

　　「沙丁魚罐頭」大概就是在描述現在的我吧。我站在火車車廂裡，忍受著從四面八方而來的擁擠壓迫，更糟的是，人們在車廂裡抽菸！到底是哪種政府會允許人民在車廂裡吸菸啊？無法置信！通勤真是每天令人絕望的事。終於下了車後，便看到蘿絲站在售票亭等我。蘿絲是我的同事，我們剛好住在同一區，因此會在同一站下車。

　　在城市裡工作並被迫每日通勤很難受，我曾想過搬到城裡，但自從發現蘿絲跟我一樣要通勤之後，我就放棄這個念頭了，這樣才能每天見到她。我們彼此打了招呼後就開始往上班的地方移動。跟蘿絲相處總讓我感到放鬆，我想她也有一樣的感覺。「嘿，你吃早餐了沒？」她突然問道，並遲疑地遞給我一個紙袋。裡面是油炸包！「我親手做的。」她有點羞赧地笑著說。真是驚喜！雖然我還不想貿然改變我們的關係，但她讓我心裡有了暖意。

● Pirozhki

This is a little bun with various fillings tucked inside. The bread is stuffed, baked and then fried. It is a convenient snack or light meal, which can be served savory as well as sweet. The stuffing is almost unlimited: from meat, egg, rice and vegetables, to fresh or cooked fruit. In Russia, Pirozhki vendors are everywhere: on the street, in the theater, train station, etc. Little cabinets enclosed with a man or woman together with piles of pirozhki producing the unique scenery of Russia. Pirozhki also has developed its variations. Around the Baltic sea area, in Finland, and in Mongolia especially.

● 油炸包

這是一種塞滿內餡的小麵包。這種麵包先填餡、烘烤最後油炸。這也是一種方便的點心或便餐，口味可鹹可甜。麵包內餡幾乎是沒有限制的：從肉類、蛋、米飯和蔬菜，到新鮮或煮過的水果。在俄國，油炸包的攤販隨處可見，不論是街角、戲院或火車站都可見蹤跡。在一個迷你的封閉空間裡，一個男人或女人和一大堆油炸包坐在一起的畫面形成獨特的俄式風景。油炸包演變出許多變化，特別可見於波羅的海地區、芬蘭及蒙古。

字彙補充包

squeeze　**v** 擠壓	what on earth...? 到底為何/怎麼回事
permit　**v** 允許	unbelievable　**adj** 無法置信的
despair　**n** 絕望	kiosk　**n** 售票亭
happen to　剛好	give up　放棄
greet　**v** 打招呼	hesitantly　**adv** 遲疑地
timidly　**adv** 害羞地	recklessly　**adv** 粗心地
tuck　**v** 塞；擠進	light　**adj** 輕盈的
vendor　**n** 小販	cabinet　**n** 包廂；櫃子
enclose　**v** 圈住；圍住	pile　**n** 堆；疊
scenery　**n** 風景	variation　**n** 多樣化

Part**1** 美食異國情緣篇

Part**2** 美食口語強化篇

unit 42

Cinnamon Roll
肉桂捲

 情緣園地 MP3 *42*

My boyfriend is an instagramer. Whenever we order something in a café or a restaurant, he never **allows** me to eat **unless** he has taken the photos he wants. I **roll my eyes**. Come on! The food is getting cold! I'm **sick of it**.

Finally, after he finishes his **photography**, I take a bite on my lovely cinnamon roll. One of the **reasons** I like it is because of the hot, sticky cinnamon **icing** on the top. "**The icing on the cake**" totally works here. Evan looks at me and smiles, then he gives me a kiss. He knows that I like cinnamon rolls, so even though he is not a sweet-eater like me, he never **complains**. Understanding this, I **appreciate** his **move** and **cherish** tea time with him. I feel like we think of each other so much, that we just **pair up** perfectly like the cinnamon roll and all its adorable elements.

　　我的男友是個 instagram 玩家，每次我們去咖啡館或上餐廳，他總要先拍夠照片才准我開吃。我翻了個白眼。拜託喔！食物都冷了！

　　終於，他照完相了，而我得以大口咬下我的肉桂捲。我喜歡肉桂捲的原因之一，是因為上頭有溫熱、黏呼呼的肉桂糖霜。「蛋糕上的糖霜」是最棒的部分，此話不假。伊凡看向我並微微一笑，然後他給了我一個吻。他知道我喜歡肉桂捲，因此雖他不是像我一樣的嗜甜者，他仍奉陪到底。我對他的體貼相當感激，也很珍惜每一次的午茶時光。我們是這麼的為對方著想，這讓我覺得我們簡直像肉桂捲和糖霜一樣，是個完美組合呢。

● Cinnamon Roll

Originated in North Europe, cinnamon roll is a dessert bread that always brings the family together. In Finland, it is **shaped** like a "**slap** on the ear", which is folded in the middle and high up on the other sides. It is usually decorated with **nib sugar** and raisin. In North America, however, a thick layer of icing is common. Besides the cinnamon itself, the icing is produced with **confectioners' sugar**, more cinnamon and drops of water. It's such an **indulgence** to enjoy the roll when it's hot and the icing is melting.

● 肉桂捲

肉桂捲源自於北歐,這是一種會將家人聚集到桌邊來的甜點麵包。在芬蘭,肉桂捲的造型像被摑掌的耳朵:中間凹陷,兩邊凸出。通常會使用珍珠糖和葡萄乾加以裝飾。然而,美國的肉桂捲常會有厚厚一層的糖霜。除了肉桂捲本身,糖霜是由糖粉、更多肉桂粉和幾滴水製成。熱呼呼地享用流淌著糖霜的肉桂捲是至高無上的享受。

字彙補充包

allow **v** 允許	unless **adv** 除非
roll sb's eyes　翻白眼	account **n** 帳戶
sick of sth.　對某事厭煩	photography **n** 攝影
reason **n** 原因	icing **n** 糖霜
icing on the cake 指某件事最好的部分	complain **v** 抱怨
appreciate **v** 感激	move **n** 行為
cherish **v** 珍惜	pair up　成對
element **n** 元素	shape **v** 塑形
slap **v** 摑；拍	nib sugar **n** 珍珠糖
confectioners' sugar **n** 糖粉	indulgence **n** 放縱

Semifreddo
冰淇淋凍糕

MP3 43

I really hope that I **pull this off**. If I don't, I'm **screwed**. I shouldn't have promised this. Lindsey is a **loyal** customer of our coffee shop. She comes in every morning, and that's how we got talking. "So you like to cook?" She looked surprised, even forgot to drink her Macchiato. I got excited and started to **boast** about myself. "I wish I could taste your meal." She **winked** at me and said. How could I turn those eyes down?

Somehow, I put myself in a very **embarrassing** situation: I promised to cook a complete Italian meal for her. Luckily, with some help from my friends, I managed to prepare an **appetizer** and the entrées. Now, the thing is the semifreddo. They are in the **freezer**, and they don't seem to be frozen! I don't want to disappoint Lindsey on our first date! "The food is **fabulous**." Lindsey wipes up her mouth and praised the food, elegantly. Then she dives into the semifreddo, and suddenly her face brightens up. "This is mind-blowing, Joe." She **giggles**. At that moment, I believe that my heart just melts in her mouth with the semifreddo. 我真是受夠了。

Part 1　美食異國情緣篇

Part 2　美食口語強化篇

　　我真的很希望能成功，如果我失敗，我就死定了。我真不該承諾這件事的。莉西是我們咖啡廳的常客，她每天早上都來光顧，而這就是我們聊起來的契機。「所以你喜歡下廚呀？」她看起來很驚訝，甚至忘了喝她的焦糖瑪奇朵。我太興奮了，竟開始自我吹噓。「真希望我能嘗嘗你做的料理。」她向我眨眨眼說。我哪拒絕得了那雙眼睛？

　　不知怎地，我竟挖了個坑給自己跳：承諾做一頓義式大餐給她吃。還好，因為幾位朋友的幫忙，我成功的做出了開胃菜和主餐。現在，問題出在冰淇淋凍糕。它們在冷凍庫裡，看起來沒有結凍的跡象！我可不想第一次約會就讓莉西失望啊！「真的很好吃。」莉西邊擦拭嘴角邊讚美，看起來相當優雅。接著她開始進攻冰淇淋凍糕，突然，她的眼睛亮了起來。「這真是太美味了！」她格格笑起來。在那瞬間，我相信我的心也跟冰淇淋凍糕一樣，在她的嘴裡融化了。

● Semifreddo

This dessert is considered a frozen mousse with some cracker-base at the bottom. The difference between semifreddo and an ice cream cake, is that semifreddo doesn't **contain** cake in its **structure**. The ingredients include sugar, cream and milk. It can be **flavored** with fruits, chocolate and syrup, just like gelato. A semifreddo is assembled **ahead** and completed in the freezer, which means that if it is not frozen enough, the structure will **collapse** and become a **pond** of milk-cream mixture. Thus, semifreddo is **conserved** in the freezer until serving time. A successful semifreddo should be creamy but not **icy**.

● 冰淇淋凍糕

這道甜點是有著餅乾基底的冷凍慕斯,與冰淇淋蛋糕不同的是,冰淇淋凍糕不包含任何蛋糕成分在內。其原料為砂糖、鮮奶油和牛奶。冰淇淋凍糕可用水果、巧克力和糖漿調味,就像義大利冰淇淋一樣。冰淇淋凍糕在組裝之後,將置於冷凍庫中完成。也就是說,若結凍不足,其結構將崩潰成一團牛奶和鮮奶油的混合液。因此,冰淇淋凍糕需置於冷凍庫中,直到上桌的那一刻。一道成功的冰淇淋凍糕該奶香濃郁,卻沒有冰塊結晶。

字彙補充包

pull sth. 成功做到某事		screwed 完蛋	
loyal **adj** 忠誠的		boast **v** 吹牛	
wink **v** 眨眼		embarrassing **adj** 尷尬的	
appetizer **n** 開胃菜		freezer **n** 冷凍庫	
fabulous **adj** 極好的		dive in 開動	
brighten **v** 使明亮		giggle **v** 輕笑	
contain **v** 包含		structure **n** 結構	
flavor **v** 調味		ahead **adv** 在…之前	
collapse **v** 崩潰		pond **n** 池塘	
conserve **v** 保存		icy **adj** 冷冰冰的	

Herring Sandwich
鯡魚三明治

 情緣園地 MP3 44

As a **local**, I just enjoy myself so much in **teasing** my **clients** about trying the **infamous** herring. Those who visit the Netherlands always have herring in mind, but very few of them really try a bite. Pete is one of them. Before he came, he **firmly assured** me that he would try the herring, but once he got to the **frontline**, he just **backed off**. Herring is actually not that bad. I am not being **cocky**, but those who try herring usually **end up** loving them.

Sometimes you just can't **judge** a thing before you taste it yourself. If it was not for Pete, I may just **cease** my **persecution**. But Pete is different – I like him. I gotta try the water, maybe I will get the fish in my net. Since I insist, Pete finally tries a bite of the herring sandwich. Seeing his wacky face makes me burst out laughing. Oh, this guy!

　　做為一個當地人，我很享受捉弄我的客人們去嘗試惡名昭彰的鯡魚。來荷蘭旅遊的人都知道鯡魚，但很少有人真的願意嘗上一口，彼得就是其中之一。他來之前信誓旦旦地說，他鐵定會吃鯡魚，但真的到了這裡時，他卻退縮了。鯡魚其實不難吃。我不是老王賣瓜，但是嘗過的人往往都大讚不已。

　　有時候你就是不能沒嘗過就有先入為主的觀念呀。如果這個人不是彼得，我可能會放棄說服，但彼得不同——我喜歡他這個人。我得試試水溫，說不定他也會煞到我。禁不起我的堅持，彼得終究咬了一口鯡魚三明治。看著他臉上微妙的表情，我捧腹大笑。唉，這個男人喔！

● Herring Sandwich

In the Netherlands, herring **peddlers** are everywhere. Due to the geographic **vantage**, herring has become one of the most known Dutch cuisines. The most common way to consume herring is to cut the fish up in pieces, and enjoy it with pickles and raw onions. Herring itself is usually soaked and **ripened** in brine, and preserved in oak **barrels**. Therefore, even though it seems raw, it's actually cooked. Herring sandwich is also very popular. The vendors usually grill the bread and the fish, then sandwich the bread with fish, pickles and onions. The unique taste of herring always leaves the eaters with an unforgettable experience.

● 鯡魚三明治

在荷蘭，鯡魚小販隨處可見。因著地理優勢的緣故，鯡魚儼然已成為荷蘭最出名的美食之一。最常見的享用方式是將鯡魚切成小塊，並與醃黃瓜、生洋蔥同食。鯡魚浸泡在鹽水中熟成，並放在橡木桶中貯存。因此，儘管鯡魚看起來是生的，其實算是「煮熟」了。鯡魚三明治非常受歡迎，小販們通常會將麵包和魚身在烤架上加熱過，並將鯡魚、醃黃瓜和洋蔥夾進麵包裡。鯡魚獨特的氣味常讓吃過的食客留下難忘的回憶。

字彙補充包

knock 　Ⅴ 敲打	urge 　Ⅴ 催促
unwilling 　adj 不情願的	local 　ⓝ 本地人
tease 　Ⅴ 戲弄	client 　ⓝ 客戶
infamous 　adj 惡名昭彰的	firmly 　adv 堅定地
assure 　Ⅴ 保證	frontline 　ⓝ 前線
back off 　後退	cocky 　adj 自大的
end up 　結果是…	judge 　Ⅴ 評斷
cease 　Ⅴ 停下	persecution 　ⓝ 迫害
peddler 　ⓝ 小販	vantage 　ⓝ 優勢
ripen 　Ⅴ 使成熟	barrel 　ⓝ 木桶

Croquette
可樂餅

情緣園地 MP3 45

I can't believe my date **ditched** me again. Sometimes I have the feeling that I'm the kind of person who **is supposed to** be **stood up**, but why me? I am not romantic, I **confess**, but I am **artistic**! Fine, I guess I'll just go home. 30 years without a girlfriend won't **defeat** me; even though I live up to every **trait** to be a "love loser", I won't give up.

I find some **leftover** mashed potato from another night in my fridge; I think I can do something to **transform** them. "You are like the olives in a sub: nobody wants to eat them." Tina, the girl I **had a crush on** when I was 13, told me this after I asked her to be my girlfriend. I take out the potatoes, fill them with mozzarella **morsels** and coat them with panko. The smell of frying these croquettes makes me happy. I **ignore** the fact that I am abandoned, and I will keep fighting. Suddenly, a message comes to my phone. Gloria **apologizes** for her **delay** and she wants to **make up for** it! Oh, I knew it!

　　真不敢相信，我又被放鴿子了！有時候我覺得，我就是注定被放鴿子的那一方，但為什麼是我？我不浪漫，沒錯，但至少我很藝術啊！算了，還是回家好了。三十年單身的生活才不會擊倒我，就算我有「戀愛魯蛇」的所有特質，我也不會因此放棄。

　　看到冰箱裡有些前晚剩下的馬鈴薯泥，我決定拿這些來做料理。「你就像潛艇堡裡的橄欖，沒人想吃。」我十三歲時喜歡上的女孩蒂娜，在我向她告白後這麼說。我拿山馬鈴薯泥，塞入莫札瑞拉乳酪塊，並裹上麵包粉。油炸這些可樂餅的聲音令我快樂。我會忽略自己被拋棄的事實，並繼續奮鬥。突然，手機接到一則簡訊：葛洛莉雅為她的遲到向我道歉，並希望可以補償我。哈，我就說吧！

● Croquette

Croquette is a dish that can be found all-over the world. The main ingredient is mashed potato; it is coated in bread **crumbs** and deep fried. The filling and sauce **vary** from region to region. In Asia, especially in Japan, the croquette is usually without the filling and served as a street food or a side dish. In Italy, it is usually stuffed with cheese and served with cream sauce. In some parts of Europe, fish and veal **ragout** are common for the filling. Croquette may be enjoyed **individually**, but it can also be served in a sandwich.

● 可樂餅

可樂餅是一項風靡全世界的美食，這道菜的主要材料是馬鈴薯泥，在裹上麵包粉後油炸。內餡和醬汁因地而異。在亞洲，特別是日本，可樂餅通常是沒有內餡的，常見於街頭小吃和配菜。在義大利，可樂餅通常有起司內餡，並搭配起司醬。在歐洲一些國家，內餡包括魚肉和燉小牛肉。可樂餅可以單獨享用，但也可以夾入麵包作為三明治。

字彙補充包

ditch sb.　放鴿子	be supposed to　應該要…
stand sb. up　讓（人）枯等	confess **v** 告解
artistic **adj** 藝術的	defeat **v** 擊垮
trait **n** 特質	leftover **n** 剩菜
transform **v** 轉變	have a crush on sb.　愛上某人
morsel **n** 塊	ignore **v** 忽略
abandon **v** 拋棄	apologize **v** 道歉
delay **n** 延遲	make up for　補償
crumb **n** 碎屑	vary **v** 變化
ragout **n** 燉肉	individually **adv** 個別地

Flat White
牛奶濃縮咖啡

 情緣園地 MP3 ▸ *46*

Sitting in the center of Woolloomooloo, Australia, I feel **weary**. A farm owner just told me that they had no **vacancy** for this season. I hide myself in a coffee shop, because the sun is making me **dizzy**.

Whatever, just give me a flat white, and I will be fine **for now**. I **text** Johnson, a friend of mine, hoping that I can stay in his place tonight. I decided not to be an **ignorant** little girl anymore, so I **packed up** and came here. I have no **regrets**, even the trip is **adventurous**.

Johnson arrives earlier than I expected. He orders a flat white too. "Now you can relax." He winks. Like the **foam** thinly laying on flat white, I like Johnson just the right amount: no more, no less.

　　我坐在澳洲伍爾盧莫盧區的中心，感到筋疲力竭。農場主人剛告訴我，這一季他們不缺人。大太陽讓我頭暈，因此我躲到咖啡館裡。

　　管他的，先給我一杯牛奶濃縮咖啡，至少這個當下我會覺得好過一點。我發簡訊給傑森——我的好友，並期待他今晚可以收留我。因為決定不再當個不諳世事的女孩，所以我收拾行囊旅行到澳洲來。我一點也不後悔，儘管旅程充滿挑戰。

　　傑森比我預想的還早到達，他也點了一杯牛奶濃縮咖啡。「現在妳可以放鬆了。」他眨著眼說。我對傑森的感情就像躺在牛奶濃縮咖啡上那薄薄一層的奶泡，不多不少剛剛好。

● Flat White

Known as one of the most Aussie things, flat white is a coffee **beverage** that can also be found around Europe and in the States. Now, its **popularity** increases **gradually** in Asia. Some claim that flat white is the Aussie name for latte, which are composed of both milk and steamed foam. However, the exact amount of milk and foam is what **distinguishes** these two. Flat white, unlike a latte, possesses less foam in general. It is said that a qualified flat white needs to maintain its latte art until the last drop. It is difficult to make it with thinner foam, and that is why many Australians are proud of their national coffee invention.

● 牛奶濃縮咖啡

以最「澳洲」的事物之一著稱，牛奶濃縮咖啡是一種咖啡飲品，在歐洲和美國也找得到。近來，其人氣在亞洲也逐漸上升中。有的人宣稱牛奶濃縮咖啡只不過是拿鐵在澳洲的別名，因為這兩者都有牛奶和奶泡。然而，牛奶、奶泡用量的不同才是區分這兩者的原因。不同於一般拿鐵，牛奶濃縮咖啡奶泡普遍較少。據說一杯合格的牛奶濃縮咖啡必須維持其拉花直到咖啡見底；這相當不容易，尤其是對奶泡不多的牛奶濃縮咖啡來說。這也是為什麼許多澳洲人對他們的國家代表咖啡相當自傲。

 **字彙補充包**

weary	adj 疲倦的	dizzy	adj 頭暈目眩的
text	v 傳簡訊	for now	當下
pack up	收拾行囊	ignorant	adj 無知的
adventurous	adj 挑戰性的	regret	n 遺憾
beverage	n 飲料	foam	n 泡沫
gradually	adv 逐漸地	popularity	n 人氣
vacancy	n 空缺	distinguish	v 分辨

47

Vegemite
維吉麥抹醬

 情緣園地 MP3 ▶ *47*

Mike **generously** applies a spoonful of Vegemite on toasted bread and enjoys it with a cup of black coffee. This **molasses** looking thing in front of me makes me hesitant, even wondering whether Mike is just **messing with** me.

Mike **insists** that Vegemite is as Aussie as he is, and he "has been having it since he was a baby". I sip on my latte and **peek** at the spread. Now that I am in Sydney, shouldn't I try something **genuine** and authentic? I can give up eggs benedict this time. Fine. Finally, I **give in**, and decide to **give it a shot**. Mike, unexpectedly, pulls me forward on the arm and gives me a quick kiss. "You won't regret it." He smiles, "Some things are worth trying. Maybe even me."

　　他豪邁的在烤好的吐司上抹上一大匙維吉麥抹醬，並和一杯黑咖啡一起享用。我面前這個黑糖蜜的玩意兒讓我遲疑，甚至在想麥可是否是在和我瞎攪和。

　　麥可堅持維吉麥抹醬跟他一樣很「澳洲」，而且他「可是從小屁孩時代吃到現在」。我邊喝拿鐵邊偷瞄那瓶抹醬。我好不容易來到雪梨，難道不該試試真正道地的東西嗎？這次我就放棄班尼迪克蛋吧。好吧。終於，我讓步了，並決定試試看。出乎意料的是，麥可抓住我的手臂使我前傾，並飛快的吻了我一下。「你不會後悔的。」他微笑道。「有些事物值得嘗試，比如說：我。」

● Vegemite

Vegemite is a yeasty spread originated in Australia. It is considered to **be related to** British Marmite, a similar food **paste**. Its flavor is **controversial**: you like it or you hate it, it is said. Despite its unique flavor: salty, **malty** and slightly bitter, Vegemite is believed to have high **nutritious** value, which includes various vitamins. The most common way to enjoy Vegemite is spread it on buttered bread. Also, it can be applied on sandwiches (as a **replacement** for mayonnaise), in pastry fillings, in casseroles, etc. Like many other spreads, various flavors of Vegemite are **available**, such as cheesy Vegemite or vegan Vegemite.

◉ 維吉麥抹醬

維吉麥抹醬是一種發源於澳洲的酵母抹醬。一般認為，它與英國馬麥抹醬（一種類似的食品糊狀製品）有關聯。這種抹醬的味道十分有爭議性：「要不愛死它，要不痛恨它」，約是這種概念。儘管其風味特殊：鹹中帶著麥芽香，並稍帶苦味，維吉麥抹醬被認為具有相當高的營養價值，特別是擁有多種不同的維他命。維吉麥抹醬最常見的食用方式，是抹在已塗了一層奶油的麵包上。在三明治吐司中也可見其蹤影（用以取代美乃滋），或是加入派餅餡料、焗烤料理中等等。就像其他許多抹醬一樣，維吉麥抹醬也有很多口味，例如起司維吉麥抹醬、素食維吉麥抹醬等。

字彙補充包

generously	adv 慷慨的	molasses	n 黑糖蜜
weird	adj 怪異的	doubt	v 懷疑
mess with	打哈哈、呼攏人	tiny	adj 迷你的
flippant	adj 輕浮的	hangover	n 宿醉
insist	v 堅持	peek	v 偷看
genuine	adj 真正的	give in	讓步
give a shot	試試看	be related to	跟…有關
paste	n 糊；膏	controversial	adj 爭議性的
malty	adj 麥芽的	nutritious	adj 營養的
replacement	n 取代品	available	adj 可取得的

Pavlova
帕洛瓦蛋糕

 情緣園地 MP3 48

The first time I saw Lilia, I thought she was an angel that came to the world. She was pure, **holy** and elegant. Sitting in the **audience**, I was completely **drawn to** her. After the **musical**, I went straight to her. "I was born to be a dancer." She smiled. "It's **in my blood**." I was **stunned**. For the first time in my 25-year life, I experienced true delight and **esteem**. Since then, I have been **seeking** the chance to talk further to Lilia. She is always busy practicing, **rehearsing,** and performing.

Yet one thing I know: she likes Pavlova. These days without seeing her, I practice making this cake **in the thought of** her. Eventually, in another public performance, I **manage to** catch her backstage. My heart is pounding. I can **barely** breathe, but somehow the Pavlova gets successfully into her hand. Lilia looks surprised. "I don't usually receive gifts from fans." She chuckles in a delightful tone. I wouldn't mind to be the first one, but what I didn't expect, is that she writes me her number. This is surreal.

我第一次見到莉莉亞時，覺得她好像仙女下凡。她既純潔、神聖又優雅。坐在觀眾席的我深受她吸引。在音樂劇結束後，我筆直的走向她。「我生來就是舞者。」她微笑道，「這在我的血輪裡。」我被震懾了。活了 25 年，我第一次體驗到真止的喜悦和敬重。自此，我不停找機會與莉莉亞深談。她總是忙於練舞、排演和演出。

然而有一件事我知道，就是她喜歡帕洛瓦蛋糕。那些見不著她的日子，我就邊想著她邊練習做這道蛋糕。終於在另一場公演之後，我在後台逮到她。我的心跳得好快，幾乎快不能呼吸；然而我還是成功地將帕洛瓦蛋糕交到她的手上了。莉莉亞看起來十分驚喜，「我不常收到粉絲的禮物呢。」她輕笑著，用愉悦的語調説道。我不在乎當第一位送禮的粉絲，但出乎我意料的是，她寫給我她的電話號碼。這真是超現實了。

美食重點介紹

● Pavlova

This is a meringue cake with hard shell and marshmallow-y, silky **innards**. It was invented **in honor of** a Russian female dancer Anna Pavlova. The cake was **inspired** by her fluffy ballet dress. This cake is part of the traditional Australian and New Zealand Christmas dining table. **Due to** the southern **hemisphere** climate, this cake is usually **preserved** in the oven after being baked, in order to protect its crispness from the **humidity**. The popular way to decorate a Pavlova is to top it with heavy whipped cream, kiwifruit, strawberries and passionfruit. Its airiness and freshness complete perfectly a big Christmas feast.

● 帕洛瓦蛋糕

這是一款以蛋白製成的蛋糕，外殼酥脆，內餡如棉花糖般絲柔。蛋糕的發明是為了紀念俄國女舞者安娜‧帕洛瓦，靈感來自她輕飄飄的芭蕾舞裙。這款蛋糕是澳洲和紐西蘭傳統聖誕大餐的一部份，因著南半球氣候的關係，蛋糕通常會置於烤箱中保溫，以避免酥脆的外殼受濕氣影響。通常裝飾帕洛瓦的方式，是在頂部放上打發重奶油、奇異果、草莓和百香果。其輕盈、清爽的滋味為聖誕大餐畫下圓滿句點。

字彙補充包

holy　**adj** 神聖的	audience　**n** 觀眾席
be drawn to　受⋯吸引	musical　**n** 音樂劇
in sb's blood　天生如此	stunned　**n** 驚呆的
esteem　**n** 尊敬	seek　**v** 尋找
rehearse　**v** 排練	in the thought of　想著⋯
manage to　成功做到	barely　**adv** 幾乎不
surreal　**adj** 超現實的	innards　**n** 內裡
in honor of　向⋯致敬	inspire　**v** 啟發
due to　因為	hemisphere　**n** 半球
preserve　**v** 保存	humidity　**n** 濕氣

美食達人得分表

美洲 --------------------------------------

- ♡ 1.藍紋起司醬牛排（美國）
- ♡ 2.炭烤肋排（美國）
- ♡ 3.炸魚條（美國）
- ♡ 4.加州捲（美國）
- ♡ 5.雞肉深鍋派（美國）
- ♡ 6.可拿滋（美國）
- ♡ 7.杯子蛋糕（美國）
- ♡ 8.蛙腿（法國）
- ♡ 9.烤蝸牛（法國）
- ♡ 10.雞肉捲（法國）
- ♡ 11.鰻魚凍（英國）
- ♡ 12.鹽醃牛肉（愛爾蘭）
- ♡ 13.玉米粥（義大利）
- ♡ 14.焗烤千層茄（義大利）
- ♡ 15.義大利餃（義大利）
- ♡ 16.德國豬腳（德國）
- ♡ 17.波蘭餃（波蘭）

- ♡ 18.起士鍋（瑞士）
- ♡ 19.約克夏布丁（英國）
- ♡ 20.串烤（中東）
- ♡ 21.果仁蜜餅（希臘、土耳其）
- ♡ 22.法式吐司（法國、德國等）
- ♡ 23.甘草糖（北歐）
- ♡ 24.葡式蛋塔（葡萄牙）
- ♡ 25.牛軋糖（西班牙）
- ♡ 26.可麗餅（法國）
- ♡ 27.烤布蕾（法國）
- ♡ 28.馬卡龍（法國）

亞洲 --------------------------------------

- ♡ 29.南餅（印度）
- ♡ 30.生魚片（日本）
- ♡ 31.納豆（日本）
- ♡ 32.滷肉飯（台灣）
- ♡ 33.肉骨茶（馬來西亞）
- ♡ 34.人參雞湯（韓國）

part 2
美食口語強化篇

♡ 35.左宗棠雞（中國）

♡ 36.小籠包（中國）

♡ 37.泰式炒河粉（泰國）

♡ 38.糰子（日本）

♡ 39.糖葫蘆（中國）

澳洲 ---

♡ 40.肉派（澳洲）

看完了也別忘了……塗鴉愛心符號喔！

一問三答　藍紋起司醬牛排 MP3 49

Q1 Have you ever tried steak in blue cheese sauce? Do you like it or not?

你們曾嘗過藍紋起司醬牛排嗎？是否喜歡那味道呢？

 Michelle
蜜雪兒

I picked up the most famous restaurant in town and the medium-rare steak was perfectly cooked. Some say that blue cheese stinks, but I know that they just haven't find the right place or they didn't have enough budget to eat at the right place. You have to have the right team to cook this or you just won't get what you want.

我造訪了城裡最有名的餐廳，那三分熟的牛排實在完美。有的人說藍紋起司味道難聞，但我知道他們只不過是還沒找到一間好餐廳，或是沒足夠預算上好餐廳罷了。餐廳一定要好，否則無法吃到夢寐以求的美味。

 Matt
麥特

The steak wasn't cheap and blue cheese sounded scary. I was afraid that I would waste my money and end up wasting the steak, too. But in the end, it came out great and the blue cheese wasn't that hard to accept; the sauce was pretty strong, but it enriched the steak.

牛排不便宜，藍紋起司聽起來也很嚇人，我擔心到頭來會花了錢又無福消受。然而，事實證明我的決定沒錯，藍紋起司也沒那麼令人難以接受。藍紋起司醬味道雖然很重，但反而讓牛排的味道更有深度。

Becca
貝卡

I shared the steak with my friend because the blue cheese sounded too much for me, and I just wanted to have a bite. I've heard that the sharpness of blue cheese would go well with the steak, but it wasn't the thing for me. The blue cheese tasted weird and I couldn't help but push away all the sauce in order to enjoy my steak.

我跟朋友共享這道菜，因為藍紋起司聽起來真的太可怕了，我想說嘗個幾口就好。聽說藍紋起司強烈的味道跟牛排很搭，但實在不合我胃口。因為起司醬味道太怪，後來我只好把醬汁全推到一邊去，否則連牛排都吃不下去。

Q2 The steakhouses – especially Barbecue Pork Ribs are pretty outstanding. What do you think about this American classic?

排餐中，炭烤肋排尤其受歡迎。你們對這道美國經典美食有什麼想法？

Michelle
蜜雪兒

Meat, in any case, is essential to human race, not to mention the golden brown, crispy yet juicy ribs. When they are coated in barbecue sauce, what else in the world can compete with it? It is important though, that this kind of heavy food go with some greens. I like to have a bunch of salad on the side, and a glass of wine.

再怎麼說，肉對人類而言都是必需品，更別說是金黃酥脆、鮮嫩多汁的炭烤肋排。當肋排裹上BBQ醬汁，世間還有什麼能與之匹敵呢？不過，這種油膩的食物一定要搭配一些蔬菜，這很重要。我喜歡搭配著大量沙拉一起吃，並配上一杯紅酒。

Matt
麥特

The ribs that are done right are the most amazing food in the world. The sizzling sound while cooking on a grill, and the smell slowly coming out is going to take you to another world. I know I'm being dedicated, but you just can't resist the glowing color and the tempting smell of some perfectly cooked ribs in front of you!

料理得恰到好處，肋排是世界上最美味的食物。當肉在烤架上滋滋作響，那漸漸烤熟的香氣可是會把你帶到另一個世界。我知道我有點誇張，但你絕對無法抗拒眼前那閃耀著炭烤色澤、香味四溢的完美烤肋排！

Becca
貝卡

I have had roasted ribs once; it was good but too greasy. In my opinion, I can have it twice a month but no more. Besides, ribs are rather expensive comparing to other kind of meat, so I don't regret that I'm not a fan of it.

我吃過一次烤肋排，的確很好吃，但太油膩了。要我說的話，我覺得一個月最多吃個兩回。而且，跟其他部位的肉相比，肋排價位較高，所以我不會因為自己不為肋排瘋狂而感到遺憾。

Q3 The United States of America has invented many premade frozen goods. Fish sticks, also known as fish fingers, are one of them. Whether you're a fan of frozen food or not, you may find it hard to resist these crunchy devils. Do you agree?

許多冷凍食品發源於美國，而炸魚條，或稱炸魚柳，便是其中之一。不論你是否喜歡冷凍食品，你很可能無法抗拒這酥脆的美食。你們同意嗎？

Michelle
蜜雪兒

Fish sticks are, if I must say, mediocre. If I am served more than two, I get bored half-way through. There's no excitement; it requires no skills. I'd rather choose chicken finger or mozzarella sticks than fish sticks.

真要我說的話，我覺得炸魚條很普通。若給我兩條以上，我吃到一半就膩了。這道菜不刺激，也不需要技術。我倒寧願吃雞柳條或莫札瑞拉乳酪條呢！

Matt
麥特

I absolutely agree on the tasty aspect. In the way of

delicacies, fish sticks can't even be considered cuisine. Yet talking about the flavor itself, these breaded sticks can easily get you hooked. They taste clean, sort of simple but delicious. When baked, the outside is crunchy, whereas the inside stays moist. When deep-fried; however, they get this hard 'n soft taste that is so addictive.

　　我在美味方面是絕對同意的。至於說這是精緻美饌，炸魚條倒扯不上邊。單純談味道面的話，這些裹了粉的魚柳真的很容易讓人上癮。它們吃起來相當新鮮，可說純粹且美味。若是用烤箱烘烤，便會形成外皮酥脆、內裡濕潤的炸魚柳。若是用油炸的，這些魚條酥脆又柔軟的口感可是會讓人上癮。

White fish can hardly be compared with tuna or salmon. They don't possess so much flavor naturally. From this point of view, I think whoever came up with the idea of breading white fish is genius. The fish is bland, but with bread crumbs and a little bit of ketchup – yum!

　　白身魚很難跟鮪魚或鮭魚相比；它們生來就沒那麼有滋味。從這個觀點來看的話，我覺得想出將白身魚裹粉的人很聰明。魚本身雖滋味平淡，但裹上麵包粉，抹上番茄醬之後，哇，真好吃！

一問三答　加州捲　MP3 52

Q4

California roll is evolved from the traditional Japanese sushi. Some people despise this weird imitation, others love it. What do you say?

加州捲是從傳統日式壽司改造而來的，有人不齒的這奇怪壽司仿冒品，有的人卻很喜歡。你們怎麼看？

California roll is super great. They are not like sushi, which is always dull and goes by the book. I don't care if people call it a bad imitation; all that matters is how it tastes. The combinations are just unlimited and I love lobster meat with caviar topping especially.

加州捲超讚。它們不像壽司往往是乏味、照本宣科做出來的。我常不按牌理出牌，而加州捲就是這樣的料理。我才不在乎有人說它是糟糕的仿造品，味道才是關鍵！加州捲有無限多組合。我特別喜歡龍蝦肉配魚子醬的組合，真是此生難忘的美食啊！

I definitely like it. Creativity-wise, it is excellent, plus the flavor is good. Sometimes sushi is boring: There's tons of rice and a tiny chunk of cucumber or crab meat. Is that appetizing? That boring taste can't satisfy me. California roll, however, triumphs on appearance and on taste. It is more colorful and more complex. I especially like avocado and fried banana; it's less expensive yet so satisfying!

　　我絕對投喜歡一票。光創意面就值得稱讚，而且味道相當好。有時候壽司很無聊：一堆飯配上一小片黃瓜或蟹肉，哪裡吸引人了？單調的味道無法滿足我。另一方面，加州捲在外表和味道上都勝出，其顏色豐富且多樣。我特別喜歡酪梨和炸香蕉的組合，既經濟又實惠！

Becca
貝卡

They have different characters, which somehow reflect their inventors. I like sushi for its simplicity; it's not fancy but it's very clean. The California roll, on the other hand, can have so many combinations! For me, I'd rather pay the same amount of money and have simple but concentrated food.

　　他們有不同的性格，在某種層面上反映了發明它們的人。我喜歡壽司的單純，雖不花俏卻新鮮。加州捲呢，則有相當多組合；價錢由高至低、味道由鹹到甜都有。對我來說，我偏好付同樣的價錢，選擇簡單但純粹的壽司。

一問三答 雞肉深鍋派 MP3 53

Q5

Just like shepherd's pie or Aussie meat pie, chicken pot pie is another hearty dinner dish. Do you find comfort in this food?

如同農舍派和澳洲肉派，雞肉深鍋派也是另一樣暖心晚餐料理。你們是否在這道菜中找到安心的感覺呢？

 Michelle 蜜雪兒

The whole thing sounds simple, but it really requires skills and balance. I've had nasty chicken pot pie before. The salty and grainy gravy was killing me, not to mention mushy and flavorless vegetables.

這道料理聽起來很容易做，但的確需要技術來平衡整道菜。我曾吃過難吃的雞肉深鍋派，肉汁既鹹又結塊，讓我很痛苦，更別說爛糊糊又沒味道的蔬菜了。

Matt
麥特

There are potatoes, carrots, peas, and chicken, all in the meaty - creamy gravy. I especially appreciate the crust on top; it gives more body to the whole dish. Some may say that the filling is too soupy and creamy. My solution is to add a dash of crushed red pepper, and serve with a good slice of bread.

派裡有馬鈴薯、胡蘿蔔、豌豆仁和雞肉，全浸潤在肉味香濃又濃郁的奶汁裡。我特別喜歡上頭那層派皮，它讓整道菜更完整。有的人認為這道菜的內餡太水又太濃郁了，我的解決方案是加入幾撮壓碎的紅辣椒，並與一片美味的麵包一起享用。

Becca
貝卡

Chicken pot pie is such a hearty dish for me that I can literary eat it every day! The creaminess comforts not only the stomach, but also heart. I love serving it with some fresh salad; it's delightful and healthy.

雞肉深鍋派是道暖心料理，我可以每天吃！雞肉派不僅餵飽了肚腹，更滿足了心靈。我喜歡跟新鮮沙拉一起吃，既清爽又健康。

Q6
The NY-originated luxurious dessert cronut has gained its fame all-over the world. Do you like it?

發源於紐約的時尚甜點可拿滋風靡全球，你們喜歡嗎？

Michelle
蜜雪兒

I visited Dominique Ansel's bakery in New York, of course, and got the real deal. Although the fake ones are everywhere, it is not comparable to the real thing! Here is my cronut experience: crispy, delicate, and beautiful. This kind of dessert suits an elegant lady like me!

我造訪了位在紐約的多明尼克‧安西烘焙坊，並享用真正道地的可拿滋。雖然仿冒的可拿滋隨處可得，但那跟真貨可沒得比。如果你想要好味道，可得尋本溯源，對吧？我的可拿滋經驗如下：酥脆、精緻、美麗。這種甜點正適合我這優雅的小姐呢。

Matt
麥特

I guess I'm not a sugar-eater... to be honest, my cronut experience is from Carrefour. They make good cronuts, though! They might not be as good as the New Yorker's deal, but it's not bad! I mean, everybody loves a doughnut, and croissants are delicious, too! Nothing can go wrong with the combination of those two.

　　我想我不是個甜食愛好者…老實說，我購買可拿滋的地方是家樂福。不過他們的可拿滋還不賴耶！可能跟紐約貨沒得比啦，但不難吃。我是說，大家都喜歡甜甜圈，可頌也很美味，這兩種的組合絕不可能差到哪裡去。

Becca
貝卡

I had my cronuts in Mister Donut, and they are pretty decent. The only fault is that sometimes the dough can be tricky and become greasy. It depends on the chef and on luck, I guess. Even in the same shop, sometimes I get a disgusting cronut, and that's horrible.

　　我都是去Mister Donut買可拿滋，他們做得不錯。唯一的缺點是，有時候麵糊不易掌控，結果弄得油膩膩。這要看糕餅師的技術和運氣了，我想。就算是同一間門市，有時候我還是買到噁心的可拿滋，這就可怕了。

Q7

It seems that a cupcake tornado started from Sex and the City. Are you also charmed by these handful delights?

似乎在《慾望城市》開播後，杯子蛋糕的旋風也隨之產生。你們是否也臣服於這些杯子甜點的魅力呢？

 Michelle 蜜雪兒

Having cupcakes in Magnolia Bakery is a must-do in New York, not only because it's featured in Sex and the City, but also because the flavor that makes it a spectacular taste. Sometimes the classic ones just can't be beaten. I do like fancy cupcakes, and my favorite is red velvet.

造訪紐約一定不可錯過蒙哥利亞烘焙坊，不僅是因其出現在《慾望城市》裡，更因那無與倫比的好味道。有時候經典口味就是最棒的。我也喜歡漂亮炫麗的杯子蛋糕，最愛紅絲絨口味。

 Matt 麥特

A cupcake can go up to $4 and that's like a burger in McDonald's. Instead of fancy yet sugary cakes, I'd rather go for savory sandwiches. As for flavor, most of the cupcakes are too sweet. The cake is buttery, the frosting is pure sugar, it almost gives me a headache. However, if I must choose one flavor, I'd say key lime.

　　一個杯子蛋糕可達售價四美元，等於麥當勞一個漢堡。要我吃個漂亮但膩人的蛋糕，我寧願選正餐三明治。至於味道，大部分杯子蛋糕都太甜了。蛋糕本身奶油味很重，糖霜又是純砂糖製成，我幾乎要頭痛了。一定要我選個口味的話，我會選萊姆蛋糕。

Becca
貝卡

However, occasionally I do like to have a cupcake as my afternoon treat. The enjoyment starts from the moment a cupcake pops up on my office desk – who can turn that down? I like my cake to be dyed with natural colors, such as beets, carrots, oranges, etc.

　　可是有時候我的確想吃個杯子蛋糕當下午茶。從杯子蛋糕出現在辦公桌上的時刻起，心情也隨之飛揚，誰能拒絕？我喜歡自然染色的蛋糕，比如甜菜、胡蘿蔔、柳橙等。

一問三答　蛙腿　MP3 56

Q8 Eating frogs' legs has been practiced for ages in France. Do you like those jumping, hopping legs on your plate?

吃蛙腿在法國已有百年歷史，你們是否喜歡那雙總是蹦蹦跳跳的腿出現在盤子上呢？

Michelle
蜜雪兒

I've only eaten one kind of frog legs: deep-fried. The breading process completely covers up the shape, which makes it more appetizing. Deep-fried frog legs are juicy, crunchy, and they go perfectly with sweet-spicy sauce.

我只吃一種蛙腿料理：油炸蛙腿。因為裹了粉的緣故，完全看不出蛙腿的形狀，感覺比較吃得下去。油炸蛙腿多汁、酥脆，跟甜辣沾醬很搭。

Matt
麥特

I had frog legs hot pot in Jakarta, Indonesia. The legs were cooked with vegetables until tender, served with rice and some pickles. I love the combination of soup and rice. It was hearty, simple, and delicious. I believe that good food always has different forms, and there's no need to set boundaries on it.

　　我曾在印尼雅加達吃到蛙腿火鍋；蛙腿和蔬菜一起燉煮到柔軟，搭配白飯和醃菜。我喜歡有湯有飯的感覺，十分暖心、簡樸又美味。我相信美味的料理形式相當多，幾乎是沒有極限的。

Becca
貝卡

I like the fact that they cook frog legs with lemon juice and parsley. It eliminates the disgusting earthy flavor that I expect to have, and the plate adds color to the dish. The dish turns out to be elegantly prepared by French chefs, and I appreciate that the legs are nicely browned on the outside.

　　我喜歡用檸檬汁和西洋芹料理的蛙腿，不僅沒有我預期的噁心土味，餐盤看起來顏色漂亮。在法國廚師的巧手下，這道料理外觀顯得優雅許多。我也很喜歡煎得焦焦的蛙腿。

Q9 Another bizarre but classic French cuisine, the crawling Mollusk: snail. Are you familiar with these tiny guys when they become your food?

另一道詭異卻經典的法式美食，蠕動的軟體動物：蝸牛。你們對這些小傢伙成為盤中飧還覺得熟悉嗎？

Okay, maybe I did have it once... accidently. It was in nice restaurant in Paris. I saw a beautiful green plate coming. I tasted it, it was like a mixture of umami and herbal sauce. I thought it was tasty. Then I asked the waiter what it was... then I almost threw up!

好吧，我或許的確吃過一次，純屬意外。當時我在巴黎一間美妙的餐館，一盤漂亮的綠色菜餚上桌。我嘗了嘗，覺得像鮮美的香草醬。我覺得還挺好吃的，就問侍者那是什麼菜…結果我幾乎吐了！

I have to say that comparing to French escargots, I prefer Asian grilled snails. I like that the fishermen just catch the snail at the coast and grill them on the spot. The sea snails are infused by red pepper, rice wine and a hint of saltiness from the sea. Asian food has bold flavor, and watching men moving their hands to catch and cook those fruits of sea is such a pleasure.

我必須説比起法式蝸牛，我偏好亞洲風燒烤螺肉。我喜歡漁夫們在海邊抓螺，並當場燒烤。這些海螺加入紅辣椒、米酒，和大海的鹹味一起料理。亞洲料理都有鮮明的味道，而看著人們舞動抓螺、料理實在是種饗宴。

Becca
貝卡

French escargot are stuffed with pesto and sprinkled with cheese. It kind of turns these creepy-looking Mollusks into another delicacy. When I see it in the form of that, although I still have to pull the flesh out of its shell, it's more acceptable.

法式蝸牛塞了青醬並撒上起司，幾乎讓這些令人起雞皮疙瘩的軟體動物變成一道佳餚了。當我看到這樣料理的蝸牛，雖還是得將肉從蝸牛殼裡挖出來，但已經比較可以接受了。

一問三答　雞肉捲　MP3 58

Q10　Roulade de Volaille, also known as chicken roulade, is a famous and common dish in France. It's spread all over Europe, and its variations develop in each country. What's your favorite chicken roulade?

雞肉捲在法國是一道有名且常見的菜餚。其蹤跡遍及全歐，在每個國家又有各自的變化。什麼是你們最喜歡的雞肉捲呢？

Michelle
蜜雪兒

It's such a classic food that none should miss out on. My ideal chicken roulade must have sun-dried tomatoes, spinach and prosciutto. I like it clean, simple, and rich. All the flavors will add up when there is prosciutto. A perfect chicken roulade needs to have a perfect crust and a juicy interior.

我心目中的雞肉捲必須包含油漬番茄乾、菠菜和帕瑪火腿。我喜歡乾淨、簡單、豐盛的感覺。只要有帕瑪火腿，所有味道都會獲得提升。一道完美的雞肉捲需要有漂亮的焦脆外層，以及多汁的肉。

Matt
麥特

Cooking chicken roulade with friends is a lot of fun, especially the stuffing part. I appreciate the version with cheese, pickles and bacon the most. There's a contrast of tanginess and creaminess that all goes well with the juice of the chicken itself. Traditionally, chicken roulade is pan-seared and baked, but deep-frying can produce this crispy skin that none is able to rival.

　　跟好友一起料理雞肉捲很好玩，特別是填料那部分。我最喜歡塞了起司、酸黃瓜和培根的雞肉捲。酸味和奶味有股衝突感，多種味道在雞的肉汁中融為一體。傳統而言，雞肉捲先在鍋中煎至上色，再烘烤完成，但油炸的雞肉捲有酥脆外皮，是難以匹敵的。

Becca
貝卡

I prefer a cheese-filled chicken roulade, with some bacon and mushrooms. For a half-vegetarian like me, I don't eat chicken roulade in search of a meaty taste. What I want in this dish is the different components with all its textures. That complexity is what attracts me.

　　我偏愛起士內餡的雞肉捲，佐有培根和蘑菇。對像我一樣的半素者而言，食用雞肉捲不是為了追求食肉感，而是醉心於相異食材碰撞出的火花；這樣的繁複口感吸引著我。

一問三答　鰻魚凍　MP3 59

Q11　The notorious jellied eel has become one of the most British dishes. Do you respect this historical dish from the UK?

惡名昭彰的鰻魚凍已成了英國最為人所知的菜餚之一。你們是否對這道歷史悠久的英式名菜敬而遠之呢？

Michelle
蜜雪兒

You wouldn't believe how frightened I was when I saw the eel body floating on the jelly with its skin on. The dish looked like leftovers that have been forgotten in the fridge. The flavor? Don't even ask. Tastes like pipe water.

你絕對不相信我看到鰻魚身體漂浮在結凍的膠狀物上，還帶著魚皮時的驚嚇程度。那盤料理看起來像被遺忘在冰箱已久的剩菜！味道？甭提了，像水溝水似的！

Matt
麥特

I've heard that jellied eel can be dated back to 18th century, when people were starving most of the time. Someone then started to catch eels from the River

Thames and cook them with limited ingredients. The result is the jellied eel we have today. I feel sad eating this dish, because eel is so delicious in other countries like Japan! Freezing tasty eel in its juice, for me that is almost a crime.

　　我聽說鰻魚凍是在十八世紀時，因為人們常處在飢餓的狀態之中，有人便開始從泰晤士河中抓取鰻魚，並與有限的材料一起烹煮。其結果便是我們今天看到的鰻魚凍。吃這道菜讓我覺得難過，因為鰻魚在日本可是佳餚啊！把這麼美味的鰻魚凍在自己的魚汁裡，對我來說簡直是犯罪行為。

Becca
貝卡

I am not crazy about the texture of the eel; it's soggy and it tastes bland. All I get in the jelly is a hint of saltiness, and not in the good way. I wish they could have developed a recipe with richer taste.

　　我不喜歡鰻魚的口感，軟糊糊的，吃起來沒味道。我在鰻魚凍裡唯一嘗到的是一絲鹹味，而這不是誇獎。要是英國人可以發明出更有滋味的食譜就好了。

一問三答 鹽醃牛肉 　MP3 60

Q12 Even if you are not Irish, you must have heard of St. Patrick's day. Corned Beef and cabbage is the tradition on this holiday. Do you enjoy the spirit of St. Patrick's day on the table?

就算你們不是愛爾蘭人，你們也一定聽過聖派翠克節。吃鹽醃牛肉和高麗菜是這個節日的傳統。你們喜歡品嘗盤中的聖派翠克精神嗎？

 Michelle 蜜雪兒

　　Corned beef has nothing to do with corn. Yes, I can read your mind. It actually indicates that the meat is preserved by salted water in a can. I am not crazy about corned beef; it has this strong flavor that I find hard to get by. Nevertheless, at least once in a year I have an eagerness to eat it. The scene of a good old pot in the kitchen always throws me back to my childhood.

　　鹽醃牛肉跟玉米沒關係（註：鹽醃牛肉的英文為corned beef）。對，我知道你在想什麼。事實上，那是指牛肉是在鹽水罐裡保存的。我沒有很喜歡鹽醃牛肉，因為它有個強烈的氣味，我不太能適應。即使如此，至少一年一次我會有股強烈的衝動要吃鹽醃牛肉；廚房裡放著個大鍋的景象總是帶我回到童年。

Matt
麥特

Corned beef by itself is not my favorite. I think it's reasonable that I go for fresh steak, right? However, I do love corned beef hash. After St. Patrick's day, there are usually leftovers. Corned beef with turnips, potatoes and carrots really creates a balanced hash. It's even better than a hash brown, I have to admit. I am certainly a big fan of that.

純粹的鹽醃牛肉我不愛。我覺得棄之而取新鮮牛排可以理解，對吧？不過，我的確很喜歡炒醃牛肉碎。在聖派翠克節過後，通常都有剩菜。鹽醃牛肉和蕪菁、馬鈴薯及胡蘿蔔共同譜出和諧的樂章。我必須承認，這幾乎比炸薯餅還好吃！我真的超愛。

Becca
貝卡

I don't like the saltiness of corned beef. Since I am not a meat-eater, it's harder for me to accept some kind of salted beef. I can have some lean parts, and that's my best effort.

我不喜歡鹽醃牛肉的鹹味。因為我不是個肉食愛好者，所以要我接受鹹牛肉比一般人更難。我可以吃些瘦肉的部分，但最多就是那樣了。

Q13 This hearty creaminess is considered an essential side dish for Italian cuisine. No matter if it's soft or hard, creamy or smoky, polenta always seems to be a crowd-pleaser. Do you feel the same for this Italian classic?

這道暖心的奶香料理被認為是義大利菜餚中不可或缺的配菜。不論是軟是硬、奶香或煙燻，玉米粥總是受人歡迎。你們也一樣喜歡這道經典義大利菜嗎？

Michelle
蜜雪兒

Polenta is not on my list of delicacies. Polenta reminds me of English porridge, and that is the food served in an orphanage. That is one of the last foods that I would eat.

玉米粥不在我的美食清單上。玉米粥讓我聯想到英式燕麥粥，那是孤兒院的伙食欸。這是我最不想吃的食物之一。

Matt
麥特

I prefer solid polenta over a wet one. When it's made with less water, it becomes more like a loaf than a bowl of porridge. It's easier to slice, grill and become a condiment on the plate. A good companion of polenta is Italian sausage. In my book; they complete each other. The sausage has a hint of anise spice that goes so well with the cheesy polenta.

　　我偏好固態的玉米粥，不喜歡液狀的。如果烹調時使用較少的水，玉米粥就會形成條狀，而非粥狀。這樣就比較容易切片、烘烤，成為美味的佐料。根據我的看法，玉米粥的好搭檔是義大利香腸，它們使彼此完整。香腸有一絲八角的味道，跟玉米粥很搭。

Becca
貝卡

It's so creamy and vibrant, and a sprinkle of herbs really brightens it up. Polenta also becomes a necessity when it comes to ragout, which is quite frequently used in Italian and European cuisine.

　　這樣的玉米粥充滿奶香，令人振奮，幾撮香草更是畫龍點睛。若提到義大利及歐陸菜餚中常出現的燉肉，玉米粥更是不可或缺的存在。

Q14 Italian food is famous for its marinara sauce and parmesan cheese. One perfect combination of the two: eggplant parmesan. Even without macaroni, this dish is satisfying, isn't it?

義大利美食以番茄紅醬和帕瑪善起司著稱，而焗烤千層茄便是這兩樣料理的完美結合。就算沒有義大利麵，這道菜還是很令人滿足，不是嗎？

It is tasty, but the way it is baked lacks fineness. Beside, that is a big portion of the same thing. You can only have so much before you get tired of it.

好吃是好吃，但是烤的方式缺少精緻度。除此之外，吃這道菜就是吃一大盤口感相同的食物，過一會兒就煩膩了。

Somehow, Italian foods all have this common point: cheese, baked, and marinara sauce. The thing about eggplant parmesan is that it looks heavy, but actually it melts in your mouth. Moreover, although the marinara sauce covers the whole thing, it's not overpowering. The secret might be the breading on the eggplant, which is a mixture of bread crumbs, Italian spices and parmesan cheese.

　　怎麼說呢，義大利菜有些共通點，那就是起司、烘烤、和番茄紅醬。焗烤千層茄看起來很油膩，但其實入口即化。還有，雖然番茄紅醬淹過整道菜，卻不會只嘗到番茄味。其秘訣或許是裹在茄子上那層混合了義大利香料和帕瑪善起司的麵包粉。

Becca
貝卡

　　I find this dish surprisingly delicious. I am not crazy for marinara sauce; I always find it either too tangy or too sweet. Eggplant parmesan, however, marries all the ingredients together. There are eggplants which are tender and juicy, crushed tomatoes with a little bit of tartness, and the creaminess from melted parmesan cheese. Although I thought the eggplant would be greasy, it is not. This is a truly satisfying dish.

　　這道菜是意料之外的美味。我不是番茄紅醬迷，它不是太酸就是太甜。然而，焗烤千層茄卻把所有食材漂亮的結合在一起。茄子既柔軟又多汁，番茄糊帶點微酸，融化的帕瑪善起司則帶著奶香。我以為茄子會油膩膩的，但事實上卻不會。這是一道令人滿足的料理。

Q15 Italians not only boast about their pizza, but also various pastas, including these little wrapped-up delights. What kind of ravioli do you like the best?

義大利人不僅以披薩自豪，更以多樣化的義大利麵為傲，包括這些小巧、令人愉悅的荷包。哪種義大利餃最令你們喜愛呢？

Michelle
蜜雪兒

Unlike linguine, ravioli don't get you messy. As for the filling, I'm not someone innovative. Red sauce and ground beef would be my choice. Classic is the best! Ravioli serves as a hearty meal for me; after a long day, a plate of red sauce ravioli and a glass of wine will revive my whole being.

不像細麵，義大利餃不會搞得你髒兮兮。至於內餡，我是沒什麼新點子啦，紅醬和牛絞肉就是我的最愛了。經典最棒！義大利餃對我來說是道暖心料理，在漫長的一天過後，一盤紅醬義大利餃和一杯紅酒會讓我整個人復甦過來。

Matt
麥特

I feel like the ravioli are another kind of pizza; you can put anything in there, and you can apply any kind of sauce on them. I especially like deep-fried ravioli. It's like a wonton with a tastier skin. The crunchiness and the sauce somehow create a harmony that you can hardly resist. For a meal, I prefer wild mushroom filling with cream sauce. For dessert, I like chocolate and banana ravioli. Surprised?

義大利餃給我的感覺是另類披薩，因為填料可以自由發揮，醬汁也可以任意選擇。我特別喜愛油炸義大利餃，感覺像有著美味外皮的餛飩。酥脆的外皮和醬汁有莫名的協調感，讓人難以抗拒。若要説正餐，我偏好野蘑菇內餡的餃子搭配奶油醬汁，甜點的話則喜歡巧克力香蕉口味的餃子。嚇一跳吧？

Becca
貝卡

I like my ravioli to be lighter. Sage pesto sauce and butternut squash filling, for example, is a perfect combination for me.

我喜歡輕盈些的義大利餃，比如鼠尾草青醬和秋南瓜內餡，對我而言，就是個完美的組合。

Q16 Schweinshaxe, as known as German roasted pork hock, is one of the most recognizable dishes in the world. How do you feel about this German pride and joy?

德國豬腳，也就是德式烤豬蹄膀，是世上最為人所知的菜式之一。你們對這道德國的驕傲有何看法？

 Michelle 蜜雪兒

I prefer roasted Schweinshaxe. Fried Schweinshaxe is a disaster: the skin is tough, and the meat is dry. Roasted Schweinshaxe, on the other hand, is juicy and pulls apart. It goes so well with German beers, so if you are a fan, this is your choice.

我比較喜歡燒烤的德國豬腳。油炸的豬腳是個災難，豬皮很硬、豬肉乾澀。相較於此，燒烤的豬腳多汁又柔軟，一碰即骨肉分離。豬腳跟德國啤酒很搭，如果你是好此道者，選這道菜準沒錯。

 Becca 貝卡

For me, this is like a "90%" meat and "10%" vegetable plate that is designed for meat-eating cultures.

Just look at this dish and you'll realize why their people are robust and strong. Normally, I don't enjoy a big chunk of meat, but I do feel more comfortable to eat it along with sauerkraut. I believe that the acid kills the meaty taste and makes it more enjoyable.

依我來看，這道菜是由百分之九十的肉和百分之十的蔬菜組成的，一看就是應運肉食文化而產生。看看這道菜，你就明白為何德國人們孔武有力。通常我是不吃這麼大塊肉的，但跟德國酸菜一起吃就沒問題。我想酸味中和了肉味，讓這道菜更可口。

Matt
麥特

This is a truly classic German type of food; it even represents the spirit of Germany. After being in brine water for a long time, the meat is tender, ready to produce its best. Roasting is one good way to cook this big piece of delicacy, but deep-frying creates another texture which is crispy. I like them both, and a bottle of Schwarzbier, German black beer, will complete this meal.

這實在是經典的德國菜，很有德國精神。在鹽水中醃製一段很長的時間後，豬肉變得相當柔軟，預備出好菜了。燒烤是料理這一塊大肉的好方法，但是油炸會產生另類口感，也就是酥脆感。我兩種都喜歡，特別要搭上一瓶德國黑啤酒，整頓飯就圓滿了。

一問三 波蘭餃 〔MP3〕 65

Q17

Apart from Chinese dumplings and ravioli, Polish dumplings, pierogi, stand out as a unique dish. Do you embrace this Polish traditional dish just like the other two?

不同於中式餃子和義大利餃,波蘭餃相當獨特。你們是否接受這道傳統波蘭菜,就像接受另外兩種餃子一樣呢?

Michelle
蜜雪兒

The filling is composed of mashed potatoes and cottage cheese, and the dumplings are garnished with fried onions. I wish there was a sauce to dip in. That would give this dish more components and tastes.

其內餡以馬鈴薯泥和農舍起司製成,餃子上以炸洋蔥裝飾。這組合不會太詭異,但滋味平淡。我希望至少有醬汁可以沾,這會讓整道菜多點元素和滋味。

Matt
麥特

Pierogi is a delicious dish to me. It reflects the diet of Polish people, which I think it's very cool. Unlike the

French, Italian or Chinese, Polish eating is all about "not being hungry." It might not be categorized as refined dining, but it certainly satisfies people's daily needs. Potatoes and cheese are very filling, thus just a few pierogi can go a long way.

波蘭餃對我來說是很好吃的一道菜，它反映了波蘭人的飲食，我認為很酷。不像法式、義式或中式，波蘭式飲食全在於「吃飽」。這可能無法被歸類為精緻美饌，但卻滿足人民的每日需求。馬鈴薯和起士很有飽足感，因此寥寥數個波蘭餃就能讓人有滿滿能量。

I would say that I like ravioli better, because there is sauce on the plate. Pierogi looks and tastes a lot like Chinese boiled dumplings, which dry up quickly if not eaten right away. What is different, though, is that Chinese dumplings usually have gravy inside, while pierogi don't. That is a huge defect. In this case, pan-fried pierogi may be more enjoyable.

我會說我喜歡義大利餃多些，因為盤子上有醬汁。波蘭餃看起來、嘗起來都跟水煮的中式餃子很類似，也就是說，如果沒有立刻吃，餃子會乾掉。然而，不同之處在於中式餃子通常包著肉汁，而波蘭餃卻無。這是很大的缺失。這樣看來，煎的波蘭餃可能比較可口。

一問三答 起士鍋 MP3 66

Q18 This is a dish that allows one to taste the essence of cheese itself. Especially on cold days, cheese fondue becomes a pleasure on the dinner table. Are you ready to dive into this pot of creaminess?

這是一道讓人品嘗起士原味的料理，特別在寒冷的日子，起士鍋出現在晚餐桌上令人愉悅。你們準備好投入一鍋香濃之中了嗎？

Michelle
蜜雪兒

My personal preference for fondue base is two kinds of cheese, unsweetened white wine and garlic paste. As for the dipping, nothing compares to two tips of medium-rare filet mignon. Cheese, beef and wine, what's better in life?

我個人偏好的起士鍋底是兩種起士、不甜白酒和蒜泥。至於沾料，沒什麼比得上三分熟的菲力骰子牛。起司、牛排和酒，生命中還有什麼比這個更好呢？

Matt
麥特

It's said that cheese fondue was invented by

lumberjacks in the mountains. Due to the cold weather and the energy-consuming labor, they need fondue as their calorie supply. Whether it's true or not, cheese fondue is definitely a rich dish. I like to use day old bread for croutons. It's economical, and it causes less crumbs. Also, unsweetened cheese goes super well with IPA beer!

據說起士鍋是伐木工在山上發明的。因著天氣嚴寒及勞力需求的工作，他們需要起士鍋作為熱量補給來源。不論真相如何，起士鍋絕對是道濃郁的料理。我喜歡用隔夜麵包做成的麵包塊，不僅經濟實惠，還可以減少麵包屑的產生。另外，不甜起士跟印度淡啤酒超搭的！

Becca
貝卡

Compared with a similar Swiss dish, chocolate fondue, cheese fondue is more accessible without doubt. There are so many things to dip, and among all of them, bread croutons and fruit are my favorite. Cheese fills one up fast, and acidity of fruits neutralizes the richness of the flavor.

相較於一道類似的瑞士料理：巧克力鍋，起士鍋不用說是較易親近的。沾料有很多，而在眾多食材之中，我最喜歡麵包塊和水果。起士很有飽足感，而水果的酸性可以中和其濃郁的味道。

Q19 Apart from fish and chips, you must also know British Sunday roast. For this traditional meal, Yorkshire pudding is an indispensable element. Do you enjoy this usually savory, plus unconventional pudding?

除了炸魚薯條，你們一定也聽過英式週日烤肉。對這道傳統餐而言，約克夏布丁是不可或缺的元素。你們喜歡這道不尋常的鹹味布丁嗎？

 Michelle
蜜雪兒

I kind of like it. It's crucial, though, that Yorkshire pudding is properly prepared and baked. If it loses its crispiness, it's nothing more than a soggy mess. The different texture of creaminess and crunchiness is what makes Yorkshire pudding stand out.

我還滿喜歡的。不過，確實的準備並烘烤約克夏布丁很關鍵。如果布丁失去脆度，就會淪為一團軟爛的漿糊。綿密和酥脆的衝突口感是讓約克夏布丁出眾的因素。

 Matt
麥特

British Sunday roast is definitely an event. Just like an

American cookout. This is the moment when family and friends all get together. I enjoy the atmosphere as much as I enjoy the food. Roasted beef is certainly appetizing: it's juicy, tender, and delicious. However, on this occasion, Yorkshire pudding is like an unwelcome guest. I usually just go back to my old friends: mashed potatoes and fries.

　　英式週日烤肉絕對是項大事。就像美式燒烤一樣，那是個聚集家人和朋友的場合。我享受那樣的氛圍，就跟我享受食物一樣。烤牛肉絕對讓人食指大動，那肉既多汁又柔軟，相當美味。然而，在那樣的場合，約克夏布丁卻像個不速之客。我還是鍾情於老朋友：馬鈴薯泥和薯條。

Becca
貝卡

I adore an alluring freshly-baked Yorkshire pudding. It's screaming for whipped cream and honey. And that's what I always do – dump the sweet elements in there and dig right in.

　　我還是很喜歡剛出爐的約克夏布丁；那布丁幾乎是尖叫著要打發鮮奶油和蜂蜜！而我當然照辦－把甜蜜的元素淋上布丁，然後開動！

 一問三答 串烤 MP3 *68*

Q20

Kebab is something we always see in a city. Wherever we are, we seem to find more than one kebab vendor. Do you find yourself drawn to its alluring aroma too?

問：串烤在都市很常見，不論身在何方，似乎都存在著不只一家串烤攤子。你們是否也常被串烤的香味吸引呢？

Michelle
蜜雪兒

It has been a long time since I had a kebab. It's certainly not an elegant food. It has nothing to do with fine dining. I don't necessarily enjoy grilled meat and the lingering smell of smoke.

我上次吃串烤是很久以前了。這絕對不是高貴的食物，跟精緻美食扯不上邊。我不太喜歡烤肉，那股煙味總是縈繞不去。

Matt
麥特

Of course. Being able to hunt and to cook with fire are two of human's basic survival skills. I believe that's why kebabs are always appealing to people no matter where they are. If you say you don't like kebab, you're lying. The smell of smoky wood, the juice of meat dripping down, and the experience of cooking food on a skewer, all lead to one word: delicious.

　　當然囉。打獵和烤肉是人類最原始的兩項生存技能，我想這就是無論在哪裡，串烤總是引人食慾的原因。如果你說自己不喜歡串烤，你一定是在說謊。燃燒木炭的氣味、滴落的肉汁，還有在鐵棒上煮食的經驗，這些全部都指向兩個字：美味。

Becca
貝卡

My favorite kebab skewer comprises of garlic, bell pepper, zucchini, and tomato. When the vegetables are charred, they become very tender and extremely juicy. Use zucchini and eggplant as a test, and you'll understand why. As for dessert kebab, pineapple and peach are perfect choices.

　　我最愛的串烤食材有大蒜、甜椒、櫛瓜和番茄。蔬菜燒烤之後，會變得非常柔軟且多汁。用櫛瓜和茄子試試看，你就知道我的意思囉。至於甜點串烤，鳳梨和甜桃都是完美的選擇。

一問三答　果仁蜜餅　MP3 69

Q21 Baklava is a well-known Greek dessert. Do you like these nutty-crunchy treats?
果仁蜜餅是知名的希臘甜點，你們喜歡這道充滿堅果香的酥脆點心嗎？

For me, it doesn't look as appealing as macaroon or cupcake. I like to have a cup of black tea with it. A bit of bitterness cuts down the sweetness to just the right amount.

對我來說，它看起來沒有像杯子蛋糕或馬卡龍那麼可口。我喜歡配杯紅茶，茶的澀味跟甜味形成完美平衡。

I have had Baklava many times. The crucial element of a good Baklava is the honey. Honey is the soul of this dessert. It fills up every layer. I like honey because it tastes way better than most of the big brands. Baklava is charming for its crunchiness. The nuts in the filling must be chopped to the right fineness yet still hold their texture. I think good Baklava is pretty addictive.

　　我吃過果仁蜜餅很多次了，要做出好的果仁蜜餅，重點是蜂蜜。蜂蜜是這道甜點的靈魂，它包裹每個夾層。我喜歡蜂蜜，嘗起來比大多數大廠牌的蜂蜜好太多了。果仁蜜餅的酥脆感很迷人，夾層的堅果一定要切細到剛剛好的程度，才能保有口感。我覺得好的果仁蜜餅挺讓人上癮的。

Becca
貝卡

　　It was quite a challenge for me to try Baklava. I think the desserts from Turkey and the Mediterranean area are overly sweet, and I've sworn off them ever since I tried Turkish delights. However, my aunt from Greece gave me this box of Baklava and I couldn't turn it down. Strangely, the more I tasted it, the more I found it attractive. Now I look forward to Easter every year, when my aunt mails me the Baklava!

　　吃果仁蜜餅對我來說是個挑戰。我覺得土耳其和地中海一帶的點心都太過甜膩了，自從我吃了土耳其軟糖之後，我就對這些甜點敬而遠之。然而，有次我希臘籍的阿姨送我一盒果仁蜜餅，而我無法婉拒。奇怪的是，我越吃越發現自己喜歡上這道甜食。現在，每年的復活節我都引頸企盼阿姨寄給我果仁蜜餅呢！

Part 1
美食異國情緣篇

Part 2
美食口語強化篇

Q22

In France, a loaf of baguette is essential on the dining table. In order to cut down the waste, "pain perdu", also known as French toast, was invented. This dish that was made of hardened baguette originally has become a fashion nowadays. What do you think?

問：在法國，一條法國麵包是餐桌上的必需品。為了減少浪費，「迷路的麵包」，也就是為人所知的法式吐司於焉誕生。這道原本以硬掉的法國麵包做成的料理，現今已成了時尚風潮。你們怎麼看？

Michelle
蜜雪兒

I enjoy going out and exploring the possibilities of it. Savory, sweet, whatever, I just love the fluffiness of the eggy toast. My NO.1 French toast is at Sarabeth's in New York. Their secret of making such soft and juicy French toast remains hidden.

我很喜歡到處嘗試新口味。正餐或甜點都沒差，我就是愛那鬆鬆軟軟的蛋香味。紐約莎拉貝斯的法式吐司是我心目中的第一名，他們做出極致鬆軟多汁法式吐司的秘訣仍然成謎。

Matt
麥特

It's kind of ironic thinking of the origins of French toast and look at how popular it is now. I was first exposed to French toast in Tokyo. The French toast was surrounded with fresh berries, accompanied by a mountain of whipped cream. Watching those tiny Japanese girls crying "kawaii" was an interesting thing, whereas eating such a pile of cream was a difficult task.

想想法式吐司的起源，再看看現在受歡迎的程度，覺得還滿諷刺的。我第一次吃法式吐司是在東京，吐司四周放著新鮮莓果，還有像小山一般的打發鮮奶油。看著那些嬌小的日本女孩尖叫著「好可愛！」是挺新奇的體驗，但要消化那坨奶油可說是艱鉅任務。

Becca
貝卡

I am a supporter of French toast. I think it's a beautiful and satisfying brunch for ladies when we want to have some indulgence. My favorite combination is fruit with syrup, and that's it. Too much sugar makes it hard to finish, which I have encountered many times.

我是法式吐司愛好者，我覺得這是當女性想要稍微放縱時，一道美觀又令人滿足的早午餐。我最愛的組合是水果和糖漿，就這樣而已。太多糖會讓整道料理難以下嚥，而很多店家都犯了這個錯誤。

一問三答　甘草糖　MP3 71

Q23 The Nordics boast about their unique-flavored candy that can't be beat. Whoever tastes it will never forget its taste. What do you feel about Salmiakki?

北歐人相當以自家無與倫比的怪味糖果自豪。無論是誰，只要嘗過就鐵定無法忘懷。你們對甘草糖的看法是？

 Michelle 蜜雪兒

This is one of the most disgusting foods that I've ever put in my mouth. It tastes like salted plastic, if I can picture how plastic tastes like. I don't understand why people call it a candy instead of a bioweapon? You may distill something really bad from it, I bet.

這是我吃過最噁心的食物之一，吃起來像鹹味塑膠，如果你能想像塑膠的味道的話。我不懂為什麼人們稱此為糖果而非生化武器？我敢說可以從甘草糖提煉出什麼糟糕的東西來。

Becca 貝卡

I associate it with American candies that have this gummy texture, and artificial flavor. It's kind of fake but salty at the same time. Personally, I don't hate Salmiakki. It's like something one must try in the Nordic lands.

我覺得那跟美國那些充滿人工香精味的軟糖滿像的，吃起來又假又鹹。我個人沒那麼討厭甘草糖，畢竟這是造訪北歐的必須體驗。

Matt 麥特

This candy is as quirky as Vegemite. It's something that the locals would love, but the foreigners will find a hard time to deal with. I have tasted different forms of Salmiakki: Salmiakki-flavored soda candy, soft candy, sugar-coated versions, etc. I think the saltiness and the chemicals in there have an effect like caffeine. Maybe that's why people like it.

這糖果跟維吉麥抹醬一樣怪，當地人很愛，外國人很難接受。我吃過許多不同形式的甘草糖，比如甘草糖口味的汽水糖、軟糖、裹了砂糖的口味等等。我覺得甘草糖的鹹味和它的成份有種類似咖啡因的效果，可能這就是人們喜歡它的原因吧。

一問三答　葡式蛋塔　 MP3 *72*

Q24 Many people fall in love immediately when they have a taste of Pastel de Nata, what about you?

很多人一吃葡式蛋塔就愛上了，你們呢？

Michelle
蜜雪兒

It's not like a typical pastry that only has a soft part; there is a hard shell protecting its gooey center. The main attraction of Pastel de Nata is the contrast between crunchy and soft, solid and fluid. The eggy aroma is another seduction like many other egg products.

不像一般甜點只有柔軟的口感，葡式蛋塔軟糊的內餡外包著硬脆的塔皮。它吸引人的主要原因，就是酥脆和柔軟、堅硬和軟糯的衝突感。蛋香是另一個吸引人的地方。就像許多雞蛋製品一樣。

Matt
麥特

Of course, Pastel de Nata meets the standard of being a prize-winner. Whether it wins a prize or simply wins the heart of a fan, this dessert is popular all-over the world. In Macao, China, people line up for freshly-baked

Pastel de Natas. The size is a bit bigger than the original one, but I like the fact that it's less sugary. However, I'm not a fan of the sticky feeling on the palate after eating it.

　　不用說，葡式蛋塔有得獎的資質。不論它是真的贏了獎，還是僅僅贏得愛好者的心，這道甜點在全球都受到歡迎。在中國澳門，人們排著長長的隊伍要買剛出爐的葡式蛋塔。這兒的尺寸稍大一些，但比較不甜，我喜歡。不過，我不喜歡吃完後舌頭上黏黏的口感。

Just like churro is a victory for Spain, Pastel de Nata is a glory of Portugal. I was amazed by the golden crust and the shiny custard filling when I first saw a Pastel de Nata. People say that we first eat with our eyes, and that's 100% true. Pastel de Nata has a seductive smell, and its color is a high note. A bite of this egg tart, and you'll realize what a simple dessert can do.

　　就像吉拿棒是西班牙的勝利一樣，葡式蛋塔也是葡萄牙的榮耀。我第一次看到葡式蛋塔時，為其金黃色的塔皮及閃耀的卡士達內餡所震懾。有句話說我們吃之前先用眼睛品嘗，這是百分之百正確。葡式蛋塔有股誘人的香味，其色澤也很出色。一口咬下這個蛋塔，你就會明白一個簡樸甜點的威力。

一問三答　牛軋糖　　MP3 73

Q25

In Europe, when thinking of nougat, Christmas bells ringing soon comes to mind. This soft, chewy confection must be a childhood memory for many. What about you?

在歐洲，想到牛軋糖就想到耶誕鈴聲。這個柔軟有彈性的甜點想必是多人的兒時回憶，你們說呢？

In order to achieve the best texture, egg whites play a crucial role. They need to be perfectly incorporated, so the nougat won't become too hard or too chewy. A Girls' nightmare is to have food stuck to our teeth, so my choice of nougat has to avoid that.

為了維持最好的口感，蛋白相當重要。蛋白需臻至完美，牛軋糖才不致太硬或太彈牙。女孩的夢魘就是有食物黏在牙齒上，所以我選的牛軋糖都必須避免這個缺點。

Nougat is one of the desserts that makes me

confused. After all, it's just a candy bar! Why bother with such luxurious packaging? Isn't it annoying to open up a delicate gift box, and find out that there are no more than some candy bars inside? The various flavors and gummy taste is definitely interesting, but in this case, I'd rather have Nature Valley granola bars.

牛軋糖是讓我困惑的甜點之一，不就是個糖果棒嘛！為什麼要包裝得那麼豪華呢？揭開精緻的禮物盒，結果發現幾條糖果棒，這不是很讓人失望嗎？多樣化的口味和彈牙的口感是很有趣沒錯，但若只是要這種口感，我寧願吃自然谷點心棒。

Becca
貝卡

Nougat is a candy bar that combines dried fruit and nuts. Egg whites are used as a binder for the texture. Usually, I only have nougat on festivals or holidays, such as Christmas. My favorite flavors of nougat are pistachio, pecan, and apricot.

牛軋糖是由水果乾和堅果組成的糖果棒，並使用蛋白來做為黏合的材料。通常我只在節慶日子享用牛軋糖，比如說耶誕節。我最愛的牛軋糖是開心果、胡桃和杏桃乾口味。

Part 1
美食異國情緣篇

Part 2
美食口語強化篇

 一問三答 可麗餅 MP3 74

Right now, it is the time for the so-called "crêpe festival" in France. How do you like this food that can be served savory as well as sweet?

現在法國正值所謂的「可麗餅節」期間。你們對這種可鹹可甜的食物有什麼看法

Michelle
蜜雪兒

I will say that the crêpe suzette is pretty fancy – especially when it is on fire. It is a table trick that can catch customers' eyes and make them come back. But the flavor? Sorry to say, it is not always as impressive as the flames.

我承認火焰可麗餅的確很吸睛,特別是著火的那幾秒。那是種桌邊秀,可以讓客人感到驚豔進而吸引顧客回流。至於其滋味如何?抱歉,倒是沒像視覺上那麼讓人印象深刻哩。

Matt
麥特

I don't feel quite comfortable dining on crêpes in a restaurant. When it comes to crepes, I want to enjoy it on the street. I think Asia has developed the best way to enjoy crêpes. They serve it savory with all kinds of combinations, and the price is good. Eating crêpes with smoked salmon and truffle may seem noble, but it's certainly not my dish.

在餐廳裡享用可麗餅讓我覺得不自在。說到可麗餅，我會覺得是種街頭小吃。我認為可麗餅在亞洲得到最好的發展，那兒販售各式各樣的正餐餡料，價格又合理。享用燻鮭魚和松露的可麗餅可能顯得高貴，但絕對不合我的口味。

Becca
貝卡

It is impossible. The soft and fluffy texture filled with fruit, chocolate and whipped cream is heaven in the mouth. I've also tried savory crêpes. Lemon chicken fingers with mayonnaise style, for instance. It was not as good though.

軟綿綿的餅皮配上水果、巧克力醬和打發鮮奶油，在嘴裡綻放的滋味簡直像天堂！我也有吃過鹹的可麗餅，例如檸檬雞美乃滋口味。不過我覺得還是甜的口味比較好吃。

一問三答 烤布蕾 MP3 75

Q27 Do you like the French classic dessert, creme brulee?
你們喜歡法式經典美食烤布蕾嗎?

Michelle
蜜雪兒

Traditional crème brûlée is made of vanilla beans, whole milk, cream and fine sugar. I want to see the vanilla seeds in there. As for the caramel, since the custard itself is pretty sweet, I like it a little bit bitter. The flavor levels should be just right.

傳統烤布蕾使用香草豆、全脂奶、鮮奶油和精製砂糖。我想看到裡面有香草籽。至於焦糖，因為卡士達本身已經相當甜了，因此我喜歡微苦的焦糖。焦苦的程度需恰到好處。

Matt
麥特

The biggest reason is that although it looks delicate, it's no more than a caramelized custard. A few bites may be nice, but a big bowl of it will probably make me sick. The French are famous for their passion for dessert, and a dessert means there is sugar. Hence, a bowl of well-sweetened custard really scares me away.

　　最大的原因是，雖然它看起來很精緻，充其量不過是焦糖化的卡士達。吃幾口可能還覺得好吃，但一整碗就讓我頭痛了。法國人對甜點是有名的著迷，而甜點等於砂糖，因此一碗紮紮實實、甜蜜蜜的卡士達真的會把我嚇跑。

Becca
貝卡

I love to have crème brûlée as a happy ending to my dining experience. In Asia, however, crème brûlée seems to be really easy to get, but the quality is questionable. Custard applied with some cream doesn't equal a crème brûlée. In my book, it has to have this perfect layer of caramelization on top, as crispy as a piece of glass almost.

　　我喜歡以烤布蕾作為美好晚餐的句點。然而，在亞洲，烤布蕾似乎非常容易取得，品質卻沒有保證。卡士達加上一些奶油不等於烤布蕾。依我來看，烤布蕾必須有上面那層完美的焦糖，幾乎像玻璃般易碎才行。

Q28

This exquisite, delicate "the girl's breasts" needs no further explanation. Do you approve of its fame, or do you disapprove?

這道考究、精緻的「少女酥胸」不須多做介紹了。你們是否認為它實至名歸？

Michelle
蜜雪兒

Needless to say, macarons are the most suitable gift a man can give. The best macarons are from Ladurée, without a doubt. This French patisserie has run over a century, and it still has the guts to make beautiful pastry. Macaron is not only a dessert; it's a symbol of fashion, luxury, and elegance.

不用說，馬卡龍絕對是男人送禮的首選。毫無疑問的，最棒的馬卡龍非拉居黑莫屬。這間法式甜點店已經經營超過一世紀，卻仍保有製作美麗甜點的傳統。馬可龍不只是甜點，它是時尚、奢華和優雅的象徵。

Matt
麥特

Macaron is a fancy thing for me. It is moist, sugary and cute. I admit that it's got a reason to be famous, but it is not that appealing to me. I like dessert, don't get me wrong. Nevertheless, a macaron is basically powdered sugar and almond flour, and flavoring. It may please your eyes, but it's certainly not exciting to eat.

馬卡龍對我來說是個酷炫的玩意兒。它濕潤、甜蜜又可愛。我承認它有理由爆紅，但是對我而言沒太大吸引力。不要誤會喔，我喜歡吃甜點。但是，馬卡龍基本上就是糖粉、杏仁粉和調味，視覺上可能很吸睛，但吃起來沒什麼刺激感。

Becca
貝卡

Whoever says that they dislike macaron would be lying. However, the price of this tiny treat is fearsome. Pâtisserie Sadaharu AOKI Paris might be a good choice for office ladies like me. I love how they blend in green tea into French dessert.

若有人說他不喜歡馬卡龍，那絕對是在說謊。不過，這道迷你甜點的價位倒是相當嚇人。對像我一樣的粉領族來說，青木定治甜點沙龍可能是不錯的選擇。我喜歡他們將抹茶融入法式甜點裡。

Q29 Among all the wheat products in India, naan is the one that stands out and makes its name worldwide. How do you like this flatbread, and how do you like it with your curry?

在印度眾多的餅之中，惟南餅突出並揚名國際。你們偏好怎麼樣的南餅，又偏好怎麼搭配咖哩呢？

The first time I tried naan bread was as a flatbread pizza. I like the crunchy edges and the elastic interior. What I like is to pull naan bread apart and dip it in butter chicken. Simple, but heavenly.

我第一次吃南餅是當披薩品嘗，我很喜歡邊邊酥脆的部分和有彈性的內裡。我喜歡把南餅撕成小片沾印度奶油雞來吃，很單純，但美味得不得了。

Freshly baked naan bread is aromatic and crackly. The sound of the bread being broken apart is the most beautiful music in the world. I'm enchanted by it, and I still remember my first naan and Indian curry experience to this day. Indian curry is soupy, spice-packed and hot. The bread is the only tool to dip and eat. Naan bread always does an excellent job by holding all the goodness on its flaky yet moist body.

現烤的南餅又香又脆，撕下麵包的聲響是世界上最美妙的音樂。我很為此著迷。到今天我仍記得第一次吃到南餅和印度咖哩的經驗。印度咖哩很像湯，香料味重，而且很辣。餅是唯一用來沾醬料的吃飯工具，而南餅總是能將美味的食材穩穩地擔在酥脆又濕潤的餅皮上。

Becca
貝卡

Among all, I love butter naan the most. When it comes out of the oven, melted butter is quickly applied on the bread, creating a shiny golden color and buttery smell. This always makes me hungry. India has a huge vegetarian population, so I just enjoy my meatless curry with the fragrant naan bread!

在所有口味之中，我最愛奶油南餅。南餅一出爐立刻抹上融化的奶油，這會在表面形成閃耀的金黃色和奶香味。我總是因此肚子餓。印度吃素人口眾多，因此我很享受吃無肉咖哩配香氣四溢的南餅。

一問三答　生魚片　MP3 78

Q30　Are you a big fan of sashimi?
你們喜歡生魚片嗎？

 Michelle 蜜雪兒

I don't eat raw food. The only thing I can possibly accept is salmon oyako don. If I pour sauce over the whole thing, I don't seem to taste the raw fish flavor, and that's what I want.

唯一我可能可以接受的是鮭魚親子丼，如果我把醬汁淋在整碗丼飯上，我就吃不出生魚肉的味道了，那正是我要的。

 Matt 麥特

Sashimi is delicate. Whenever I eat it, I cherish every bite. This is something you cannot cut your budget off, because cheap sashimi can cause serious disease. In my opinion, sashimi is the only way to taste the sweetness in a shrimp. Shrimp is no question my favorite item. The combination of wasabi and soy sauce creates a perfect tango in your mouth.

生魚片很細緻，每次品嘗，我總是細細品味。在生魚片上不能

省錢，因為便宜貨可能會帶來嚴重的疾病。依我來看，生魚片是唯一能吃到蝦子鮮甜味道的方式。蝦子無庸置疑是我最喜歡的食材，而山葵和醬油則在口中形成完美節奏。

Becca
貝卡

I selectively like sashimi. Salmon, tuna, shrimp are the basic items. I don't like octopus; it is one of the weirdest seafood to eat raw. Sashimi recalls me of tartare. I had beef tartare and horse tartare before, and they taste quite different from the raw food point of view. With raw onion, egg yolk and spices, the tartare dish is a new interpretation of sashimi. I think food is at its best when it's done right.

　　我選擇性的喜歡生魚片。鮭魚、鮪魚和蝦子是基本品項。我不喜歡章魚，那是最怪異的生食海鮮之一。生魚片讓我想到韃靼料理，我吃過韃靼牛肉和韃靼馬肉，以生肉的觀點來看，它們的滋味還挺不同的。搭配生洋蔥、蛋黃和香料，韃靼料理是生魚片的另一種詮釋。我覺得食物只要料理得好就會好吃。

 一問三答 納豆 MP3 *79*

Q31 Nattō is made from fermented soy beans, and the fermentation has given nattō a really special texture and smell. Even among Japanese, nattō is a food that arouses controversy. What do you think?

納豆是由發酵的黃豆製成，發酵後，納豆產生了相當特殊的口感和氣味。就連對日本人來說，納豆都是引起爭議的食物。你們覺得呢？

Michelle
蜜雪兒

The first and only time I had nattō was from a breakfast buffet. I ate it directly without knowing what it was. The result? An exile of nattō from my food list permanently.

我第一和唯一一次的納豆是在早餐自助餐，我不知道納豆是什麼，就直接放進嘴裡。結果？永久從我的食品清單上驅逐納豆。

Becca
貝卡

In the past, the Japanese emperor used to ban meat-eating; during those years, soy bean certainly provided essential nutrients. From time, to time, I put nattō in a sushi roll. This not only covers up the smell of nattō, but also transforms it into a handy, tasty food.

從前日本天皇曾禁止食肉，在那些年間，黃豆無疑是提供了必要的營養素。有時候我會把納豆包進壽司卷裡，這不僅掩蓋了納豆的氣味，更將之轉變成一種便利、美味的食物。

Matt
麥特

Nattō is something hard to be crazy about; actually, it is notorious. Although it has high nutrient value, for most of us, it's still hard to embrace. I've found two different ways to enjoy this sticky devil. The first way is to add soy sauce to it, mix in raw egg and pour on rice. The second way is to put nattō in a curry. The spice balances out, or simply covers up, the strong taste of nattō.

納豆很難討人喜歡，事實上，它臭名遠播。雖然納豆營養價值高，對大多數人而言還是難以接受。我找到兩種享受這種黏糊糊的食物的方法，一是加入醬油和生蛋並倒在飯上，二是把納豆加入咖哩中。香料的味道會中和掉納豆——或乾脆掩蓋掉——那股強烈的味道。

一問三答　滷肉飯　[MP3] 80

Q32

Chinese food is of the kind that you can smell miles away. Minced pork rice is one of them. For ages, a pot of minced pork is a definite killer way to eat rice. Are you also dying for a good bowl of meaty yumminess?

中國菜是那種從數哩外就能聞到味道的料理，而滷肉飯更是其中之一。長久以來，一鍋滷肉絕對是白飯殺手。你們也對一碗美味的滷肉飯垂涎不已嗎？

Michelle
蜜雪兒

The Chinese believe that some fat helps elevate the flavor;thus, after a long time simmering on a stove, the result is a pot of sticky and fragrant pork stew. It's an addictive dish, I'd say, which is tasty and guilty at the same time. To prevent myself from eating too much richness, I always have blanched vegetables on the side.

中國人相信油脂會提升味道，因此長時間在爐上燉煮之後，結果是一鍋黏稠且芬芳的滷肉。我會説這道料理令人上癮，美味的同時充滿罪惡感！為了不讓自己吃太肥，我通常會搭配清燙蔬菜。

Matt
麥特

I enjoy eating on a street vendor seat and being surrounded by local people. The feeling of eating like a local is the spice of traveling, and my motto of finding good food is to always follow the crowd. I especially like the yellowish pickled daikon on the rice; it reminds me of rustic farmer food.

我很享受在路邊攤被當地人圍繞著吃飯，吃得像當地人乃是旅行的提味香料，而我的座右銘便是循著人潮找美食。我特別喜歡飯上那片黃色的醃蘿蔔，很有樸實農夫菜的風格。

Becca
貝卡

The aroma of pork, garlic and shallots burst out, creating a "delicious" signal in my brain. In a few seconds, I found myself having emptied the bowl and wanting for more. Just be conscious when you dine on this dish, because it'll make you eat more rice than you really need!

豬肉、大蒜和紅蔥頭的香氣併發，在腦中產生美味的訊號。數秒之後，我發現自己將碗中飱一掃而空，還想再來一碗！吃這道料理要當心，因為它可能使你吃下很多很多飯！

Q33 Bak kut the is the Chinese pronunciation for pork in the tea. This interpretation of pork products may seem shocking to westerners. How does it sound to you?

肉骨茶是中文發音，意謂茶裡的豬肉。這道豬肉料理可能會嚇到很多西方人，你們怎麼看？

 Michelle 蜜雪兒

I'm not crazy about bak kut the because it's not visually appealing, but I do get the unique flavor profile of this dish. The tender ribs are flavorful and go well with hot sauce.

我是沒有很喜歡肉骨茶啦，因為看起來不特別好吃，但我的確感受到這道菜獨特的個性。柔軟的肋排很有滋味，沾點辣醬很對味。

 Matt 麥特

I'm a big fan of bak kut the. I think it's smart to char the ribs and cook them in Chinese spice-infused broth. For me, it's a success. I can tell that the umami flavor penetrates the meat; the broth surely does its job by simmering for a long time.

　　我很喜歡肉骨茶。將煎過的豬肋排放在加了中國香料的高湯裡煮，我覺得很妙。對我來説，這道菜很成功。我嘗得到肉裡的鮮味，那跟長時間在高湯裡熬煮有關係。

Becca
貝卡

Thanks to a time-consuming cooking process, the pork releases its flavor into the broth and actually gives some depth to it. The ribs, after being cooked for a long time, are super tender and not as meaty. I enjoy that.

　　長時間的熬煮過程，豬肉的滋味被完全釋放到湯裡，這給了湯頭深度。豬肋排在燉煮之後，變得極為柔軟而肉味不那麼重。我很喜歡。

 一問三答　人參雞湯　

Q34 This traditional Korean dish is a must-eat for those who seek for the spirit of Korean cuisine. Do you find that spirit in your pot of Samgyetang?

問：這道傳統韓國菜是對韓國精神有興趣的人必嘗的料理。在你們的人參雞湯裡，是否有大韓精神呢？

 Michelle 蜜雪兒

Samgyetang is a dish that combines soup, rice and meat all in one pot. I couldn't have more respect and gratitude for the creator of this recipe. The chicken, stuffed with rice and spices, is melt-in-the-mouth tender. Every piece of meat is soaked with its own broth. Not to mention the rice, which picks up the umami flavor of the chicken in every grain.

人參雞湯是一道結合了湯、飯和肉的料理，我對這道菜的發明者充滿尊敬和感謝。雞肉裡塞滿了米飯和香料，幾乎是入口即化。每塊肉都浸泡在雞湯裡，更別說是粒粒吸飽了湯汁、味道鮮美的米飯了。

 Matt 麥特

This Korean dish is like a root deeply planted in its

people. I like the fact that I'm able to taste all those spices in the soup, as well as the spice-infused rice. Some places serve a whole green chili alongside. I tried to eat the raw pepper with Samgyetang, and boy, was that spicy!

韓國料理就像根一樣深深扎在韓國人裡面。我很喜歡嘗得到香料味的湯頭，還有帶著香料味的米飯。有些地方還會附上整條青辣椒，我試著跟人參雞一起吃，哇，實在有夠嗆！

Becca
貝卡

Samgyetang is not just about the chicken and the rice. It is more about the kimchi and pickled veggies that come along with it. In Korea, kimchi and pickled veggies are daily necessities. Therefore, plates of kimchi are common side dishes in restaurants. What is better, they are free! I like seaweed with sesame, kohlrabi and daikon relish.

人參雞湯不只有雞肉和米飯，還包含泡菜及其他隨之上桌的小菜。在韓國，泡菜和醃漬菜是每日必須品。因此，一盤盤的醃漬菜是餐廳常見的配菜。更棒的是，小菜是免費的！我很喜歡芝麻海帶、大頭菜和醃白蘿蔔。

一問三答　左宗棠雞

Q35 Do you find General Tso's chicken tasty?
你們覺得左宗棠雞好吃嗎？

Michelle
蜜雪兒

General Tso's chicken meets every factor I know about Chinese food. It's greasy, heavy-handed, and oily. It's not like Italian dishes, which are creamy, or French dishes, which are delicate. Chinese food tends to use a lot more oil for sautéing, and an oven is usually excluded. For me, general Tso's chicken and its fame is a mystery.

左宗棠雞符合每項我印象中的中國菜會有的特徵：油膩膩又重鹹。不像奶香濃郁的義大利菜，也不像精緻的法是料理，中國菜總是用過多的油去烹調食材，而且他們好像不懂得用烤箱。左宗棠雞和其人氣對我來說是個謎。

Matt
麥特

I'm in love with General Tso's chicken. Yes, it's greasy and heavy, but it's also addictive! The balance of sweetness and savory points is spot-on, and the chicken is just cooked to perfection. This is the dish I will miss once in a while, and when I do, I must get it to kill the craving.

我超喜歡左宗棠雞！沒錯，的確又油又重鹹，但同時也很讓人上癮！甜鹹平衡的感覺很棒，雞肉也煮得恰到好處。這是我偶爾會想念的料理，而當我想吃時，我一定得吃到！

Becca
貝卡

This is basically a dish of fried chicken coated with a sweet and savory sauce. Soy sauce, sesame oil and hoisin sauce are common components. I like it just for the first few pieces, and after that my palate is exhausted. I usually have 3/4 box of chicken left in my dish when I finish the meal. Despite its good flavor, this is not the dish you want to dive in and bury yourself in there.

基本上這是炸雞裹上甜鹹醬汁的料理，醬油、香油和海鮮醬很常被拿來料理。剛吃幾塊我還喜歡，但很快味蕾就疲乏了。通常吃飽後，我的盤裡還會剩下四分之三的雞肉。味道好歸好，這不是一種讓我想一直吃下去的料理。

Q36 what do you think about Din Tai Fung's xiaolongbao?
你們對鼎泰豐小籠包的看法是？

 Michelle 蜜雪兒

I have been there once and I have to say it has turned me. But these xiaolongbao – they are incomparably good. It is not just about the gravy in my opinion, but the perfect proportion of the meat and skin is what it makes the flavor of Xiaolongbao a success.

我去用餐過一次，而我必須說真是顛覆了我的想法。不過這些小籠包啊⋯它們可是無法比擬的美味。在我來看，重點還不只是肉汁，而是皮和內餡的完美比例，造就了這些小籠包的美味。

 Matt 麥特

The way it is served – shredded ginger and a little bit of soy sauce and vinegar, is probably the secret to making it tastier. Although it looks kind of bland, somehow you just can't help but eat one after another. It is almost magical. Maybe this is the charm of Chinese food!

　　薑絲、幾滴醬油和醋大概是讓小籠包更美味的秘密。雖然這些包子外表並不起眼，但就是會無法控制的一個接一個吃下去。簡直像著魔一樣呢！也許這就是中式菜餚的魅力吧。

Becca
貝卡

Din Tai Fung has taken this civilian dish to another level. It is delicate, specific, and well-designed. Whoever has been there can testify thatthe astonishment of the gravy bursts in your mouth is an indescribable experience. These dumplings have the charm to have one taste after another.

　　鼎泰豐卻把這種平民小吃帶入另一個層次。這些包子精緻、規格嚴謹、設計獨到。只要是去過的人都可以見證，肉汁在你嘴裡爆開時的驚喜，是絕非筆墨所能形容；這些包子會讓你一直想再回去品嘗它的美味。

Q37 Pad Thai is an iconic Thai cuisine. It has gained its fame all-over the world. What do you think about this fried rice noodle dish?

泰式炒河粉是極具指標性的泰國菜，聞名全球。你們怎麼看這道炒河粉料理？

Michelle
蜜雪兒

I am not a big fan of spicy food. It's weird to pay and suffer, isn't it? The first time I got "authentic" Pad Thai, I was furious. It was inedible! Moderately spicy is acceptable, but too much isn't right. I like my Pad Thai with just a little bit of chili, and extra palm sugar. The caramelization on the noodles just tastes fabulous.

我不喜歡嗆辣的食物。花錢受罪豈不是很奇怪？第一次吃到號稱道地的泰式炒河粉時，我超生氣的。那簡直不能吃啊！適度的辣可以接受，但太辣就不對了。我喜歡加入一丁點辣椒、多一點椰糖的泰式炒河粉；河粉上的焦糖口感真是太美妙了！

Matt
麥特

In Bangkok, there are so many Pad Thai peddlers,

but very few of them serve bad food. Classic flavor: shrimp with fish sauce, bean sprout and chili is my favorite. I prefer sitting in the open air. There, I am more at ease. Also, I don't only enjoy the food, but seeing the people. It's very exotic.

在曼谷，炒河粉的攤販很多，但僅有少數會供應難吃的食物。經典口味：蝦子配魚露、豆芽菜和辣椒是我的最愛。我偏好坐在露天座，感覺很自在。在享受食物的同時，我還能看看路邊的人。這是相當異國風情的體驗。

Becca
貝卡

I'm kind of concerned about eating on the side of the road. People say that it's genuine, but I got diarrhea once. Since then, for my own good, I only eat in the stores that look clean. I like the crushed peanuts on Pad Thai. It's not crunchy, but it's aromatic. Also, I love the rice noodles. The chewiness is found nowhere else.

我對坐在路邊吃飯有疑慮。大家都說這樣比較道地，但是有一次我卻拉肚子。自那次之後，為了我自己好，我只在看起來乾淨的小店吃飯。我喜歡泰式炒河粉上面的花生碎，吃起來不會卡滋卡滋的，但是很香。還有，我好愛河粉喔。那有嚼勁的口感別處可找不到啊。

Q38
Without dango, many Japanese holidays would lose their charm and joyousness. Are you fans of these sticky rice balls?

若是少了糰子，許多日本的節日都要失去色彩了。你們是這些糯米丸子的粉絲嗎？

Michelle
蜜雪兒

Basically, dango is made of sticky rice powder and water. Then it's boiled and coated with condiments such as Anzuki bean paste, flavored sugar or sauce. Dango itself doesn't really have any flavor. Nobody likes to chew on a gummy ball, I believe. Hanami dango, however, do have beautiful colors. They are literary made for sakura-watching.

基本上，糰子是用糯米粉和水製成，之後水煮並裹上紅豆泥、調味砂糖或醬汁。糰子本身沒什麼味道，而我想沒人會喜歡一個嚼不爛的米糰吧！不過呢，花見糰子的顏色的確很漂亮。它們真的是為賞櫻花而生的。

Matt
麥特

I like it because I don't necessarily need a soft and

fluffy dessert. Rather than that, I like food that has character. Dango certainly achieves that. I prefer kinoko dango, which is a soy bean powder coated dango. It's usually slightly sweetened, and the aroma of soy bean just bursts in your mouth. I enjoy it with a cup of matcha.

　　我喜歡糰子，因為我覺得甜點不一定要軟綿綿的。與其如此，我到偏好有個性的甜點。糰子相當有個性。我喜歡黃豆粉糰子，也就是裹上黃豆粉的糰子。通常會稍帶甜味，黃豆的香氣直衝腦門！我喜歡配杯抹茶一起吃。

Becca
貝卡

Dango is usually served on a bamboo skewer, and that makes it easy and elegant to eat. I like soy sauce soaked dango. It's a sauce made of soy sauce and sugar, and it's thickened to let it sit on the dango. It doesn't taste like plain sugar, which I think is a twist on a traditional dessert.

　　糰子通常以竹籤串成，這樣既方便吃，又能吃得優雅。我喜歡醬油糰子。這是一種用醬油和砂糖製成的醬汁，並勾芡得厚厚的好裹在糰子上。這嘗起來不同於純砂糖，我覺得對傳統甜點是一種創新。

Part 1 美食異國情緣篇

Part 2 美食口語強化篇

Q39 They may look red and spicy, but they are as sweet as sugar pie. In Beijing, these crystalized candy fruit sticks are everywhere. Are you ready for a sugary punch?

它們看起來鮮紅，好像很辣，但其實跟甜心派一樣甜蜜。在北京，這些裹糖霜的水果糖到處皆有。你們準備好接受砂糖衝擊了嗎？

Michelle
蜜雪兒

Tanghulu needs to be kept under a certain temperature. If it gets too warm, the coating will start to melt and thus creating a sticky texture. It's super unpleasant to the palate. To make sure I always get a perfect and crispy tanhulu, I only enjoy them in restaurants.

糖葫蘆需要被保存在特定的溫度下，如果太熱，外層的糖晶會融化，吃起來就會黏黏的。那感覺很糟！為了保障我吃到完美、酥脆的糖葫蘆，我只在餐廳點來吃。

Matt
麥特

The traditional one is made of Chinese hawthorn, but

nowadays the variations are fancier. I like stuffed tomato preserves; they are savory and sweet. Tanghulu used to be sold only in winter, but now they are sold all-year round. They are at their best in winter, though, because the heat will melt down their crispy sugar coat.

傳統糖葫蘆使用仙楂，但今天各種水果都有。我喜歡蜜餞番茄，嘗起來甜甜鹹鹹的。糖葫蘆以前只在冬天販售，但現在四季都找得到。我想還是冬天買最好，因為暑氣會把糖葫蘆外層的結晶糖融化掉。

Becca
貝卡

Tanhulu reminds me of candy apples. The vivid color and the sweetness seemed to enhance the happy feeling. Tanhulu has the same effect. However, as tanhulu vendors increase, it seems harder to find the genuine ones. The perfect ratio of sugar coating and the balance with fruit is a science, it can't be messed up.

糖葫蘆讓我聯想到焦糖蘋果。那亮麗的顏色和鮮明的甜味增添了歡樂氣氛，糖葫蘆也有類似的效果。然而，雖然現在糖葫蘆小販增加了，感覺卻越來越難找到真正的糖葫蘆。砂糖和水果的比例是項科學，那可不能亂做啊！

 一問三答　肉派 MP3 88

Q40

People say that if you've never tried meat pie more than once, you can't be called an Australian. Can you talk about your feelings about this typical Australian cuisine?

有人說如果你沒吃過一次以上的肉派，你可不能說自己是澳洲人。你們對這個典型澳式美食的看法如何？

Becca
貝卡

It is curious for me that meat pie is actually an Australian thing. For me, it looks pretty British. I think it is rustic enough – simple, filling, a taste of earthiness.

我倒是很驚訝肉派是個澳式美食，我覺得還挺英式的呢。我認為肉派相當平庸，就是簡單、飽足，一種平凡的滋味。

Matt
麥特

I love pie that is topped with mashed potato and bean paste. It's different from shepherd's pie; it's simpler and lighter. To some people, holding a gravy-bursting bowl in one hand while feasting with the other may seem troublesome, but I think I'm just a street food nut.

　　我吃過一種在派上面疊了馬鈴薯泥和豆子泥的肉派，跟牧羊人派相當不同。這種派更單純，對身體較無負擔。可能對有的人來説，手裡捧著個會噴肉汁的派相當不容易食用，但我就是愛這種街頭小吃。

Sorry to say, but meat pie is not on my food list. I admit that it's hard to make it poorly, but it's even harder to make it impressive. The three elements of a good meat pie are: properly seasoned beef, gravy and a perfect crust. Any of it fails, start over again!

　　不好意思，我認為肉派根本不在我認知的美食範圍內。我承認要做得難吃不容易，但要做得好吃更難。一個好的肉派需要三個元素：適度調味的牛肉、肉汁和一個完美的派皮。要是其中之一沒達到標準，最好砍掉重練哦！

─生活英語─

用故事區分，以及介系詞的"功能概念"分類，搭配圖解例句，考試不再和關鍵分數擦身而過，也是閱讀、寫作與口說的必備用書！

書　系：Leader 048
書　名：圖解介系詞、看故事學片語：第一本文法魔法書
定　價：NT$ 360元
ISBN：978-986-92856-7-4
規　格：平裝/320頁/17x23cm/雙色印刷

獨家吵架英語秘笈大公開！精選日常生活情境＋道地慣用語，教你適時地表達看法爭取應得的權利，成為最有文化的英語吵架王！

書　系：Learn Smart 064
書　名：冤家英語（MP3）
定　價：NT$ 360元
ISBN：978-986-92855-6-8
規　格：平裝/304頁/17x23cm/雙色印刷/附光碟

享受異國風光，走訪知名美食熱點；帶著情感品嚐美食，才是人間美味；用英語表達富情感意涵的美食，才算得上是『食尚』。

書　系：Leader 050
書　名：餐飲英語：異國美食情緣(MP3)
定　價：NT$ 369元
ISBN：978-986-92856-9-8
規　格：平裝/288頁/17x23cm/雙色印刷/附光碟

學新語言，從髒話學起最快！罵得好，顯得有學問；但只會罵那一兩句就遜掉了！讀完這本，保證讓你掌握髒話的精準用詞！

書　系：Leader 043
書　名：學校沒有教的「髒」英文（附MP3）
定　價：NT$ 360元
ISBN：978-986-92856-2-9
規　格：平裝/288頁/17x23cm/雙色印刷/附光碟

網路購物新時代，你需要迅速掌握網購要訣！以圖解式呈現"網購"介面，使用說明中英對照；靠自己精打細算購買商品，同步練英文！

書　系：Leader 046
書　名：現學現用的Smart網購英文
定　價：NT$ 349元
ISBN：978-986-92856-5-0
規　格：平裝/288頁/17x23cm/雙色印刷

四大篇撼動人心的發明人物故事，帶領你見證劃時代的影響力。從發明家的身上偷師，提升表達力與翻譯能力，英文寫作無限飆升！

書　系：Leader 045
書　名：影響力字彙（MP3）
定　價：NT$ 380元
ISBN：978-986-92856-4-3
規　格：平裝/304頁/17x23cm/雙色印刷/附光碟

每日一句經典台詞，輕鬆摺英語！歡樂看動畫電影，輕鬆學習美式英語！額外補充意義相仿的新穎的說法，讓說話的內容不單調。

書　系：Learn Smart 060
書　名：看動畫瘋美式英語：魔鏡魔鏡，救救我的Chinglish!（MP3）
定　價：NT$ 379元
ISBN：978-986-92855-3-7
規　格：平裝/304頁/17x23cm/雙色印刷/附光碟

Leader 050

餐飲英語: 異國美食情緣 (附 MP3)

作　　　者	陳怡歆
發 行 人	周瑞德
執行總監	齊心瑀
企劃編輯	陳韋佑
校　　對	編輯部
封面構成	高鍾琪

內頁構成	菩薩蠻數位文化有限公司
印　　製	大亞彩色印刷製版股份有限公司
初　　版	2016 年 9 月
定　　價	新台幣 369 元
出　　版	力得文化
電　　話	(02) 2351-2007
傳　　真	(02) 2351-0887
地　　址	100 台北市中正區福州街 1 號 10 樓之 2
E - m a i l	best.books.service@gmail.com
網　　址	www.bestbookstw.com

港澳地區總經銷	泛華發行代理有限公司
地　　　　址	香港新界將軍澳工業邨駿昌街 7 號 2 樓
電　　　　話	(852) 2798-2323
傳　　　　真	(852) 2796-5471

國家圖書館出版品預行編目資料

餐飲英語 : 異國美食情緣 / 陳怡歆著. --
初版. -- 臺北市 : 力得文化, 2016.09面 ;
公分. --（Leader! ; 50）
ISBN 978-986-92856-9-8(平裝附光碟片)
　1.英語 2.餐飲業 3.讀本

　805.18　　　　　　　105014681